LOVE OF THE WITCH

WITCHES OF KEATING HOLLOW, BOOK 6

DEANNA CHASE

ABOUT THIS BOOK

Welcome to Keating Hollow, the enchanted village full of love, magic, and second chances.

Hope "Luna" Scott just wants a new life. After growing up in a round robin of foster homes, she has no family or ties to anyone... until she moves to Keating Hollow and starts to get close to the Townsend sisters. But Luna has secrets that could ruin everything, and when the man who broke her heart three years ago shows up, there's a whole lot more than just her heart that's on the line.

Chad Garber has lost everything that was ever important to him. Now he's back in Keating Hollow, trying to start over. But when he finds the girl he couldn't save three years ago, he needs to confront his past and make a few things right... if she'll let him.

CHAPTER 1

*L*una Scott sat at a table in the back of Incantation Café, her eyes watering from exhaustion while she sipped on her latte. It had been three days since she'd gotten any sleep, and she was subsisting on sugar and caffeine.

"Need a refill?" Hanna Pelsh asked.

Luna glanced up at the gorgeous woman and gave her a sharp nod. "Make this one a double, and can you bring another cinnamon cream cheese scone?"

"Of course." The co-owner of the café gave her a worried glance. "Are you all right? You look kind of pale."

"I'm fine." Luna waved a hand. "Just a little sleep deprived. Gotta get it together before my first appointment." Luna was a massage therapist at A Touch of Magic, Keating Hollow's luxury day spa.

"You look like you could use one yourself." Hanna sat down across from her. "What's up? Working too hard? I'm sure Faith would understand if you need a day off to recharge." Hanna was best friends with Luna's boss, Faith Townsend, the owner of A Touch of Magic. She gave Luna a conspiratorial smile. "I could tell her I need you for a girls' day. I have been meaning to take you out to lunch, like a thank you of sorts."

Luna's face heated, and she silently chastised herself for her embarrassment. She knew she had nothing to be uncomfortable about, but it still felt strange for anyone to look at her and see anything other than a major screwup. "You don't need to thank me, Hanna. You know that. I just did what any decent person with my abilities would do."

"Well, you're also renting my house. That in and of itself is huge." She winked. "My insurance company was getting antsy with it empty, and my only other applicant was that guy from Eureka who smells like fish."

Luna chuckled. "Wasn't he a fisherman?"

"Yeah, but he made my eyes water. All I could think about was that stench seeping into the walls." She made a face and shuddered, but then she smiled. "Meanwhile, you'll probably make the place smell like vanilla and lavender."

"That's the truth," Luna said, as a yawn overtook her again. She was a massage therapist who wasn't shy with the scented oils.

"Let me get you that double latte you asked for." Hanna popped up and strode back to the café's counter.

"Don't forget the scone," Luna called after her.

"Rough day?" a woman with a rich voice asked.

Luna glanced up and spotted the red-headed beauty that managed the town's chocolate shop. She was dressed in a form-fitting red top, a black pencil skirt, and red suede boots. Everything about her screamed sophistication. Meanwhile, Luna wore threadbare jeans and a stained T-shirt that had the words *Sassy Unicorn* scrolled across the chest. Luna gave her a ghost of a smile. "Hey, Shannon."

The gorgeous woman sat across from her, a paper coffee cup in her hand. "You look like hell."

"Thanks." Luna gave her new friend a half-hearted grimace. Shannon was the one person in town that Luna had really connected with. She liked Faith and Hanna. Both were sweet women, but Shannon had a cynical side that matched Luna's.

"You need a day off," Shannon said.

"I need to find time to move into Hanna's house."

Hanna chose that moment to arrive with the double latte and scone. After placing them in front of Luna, she dropped her hands to her hips and frowned. "Need an extra pair of hands? I could help you pack after I get off work."

"Nah. Most of my stuff is already packed. I just need to find a day to move it. Thanks, though." The truth was, Luna didn't actually have very much stuff. Just a couple of duffle bags full of clothes and a few pieces of furniture. "What I really need is a truck. And some muscle."

"Well, I know someone who fits that bill," Hanna said. And then, as if on cue, both Hanna and Shannon turned and looked across the café.

Luna followed their gaze and went cold all over when she spotted the object of their attention. "No. Absolutely not. I can't—"

"You can," Shannon said, cutting her off. "He's the helpful, do-gooder type."

"And he has a truck," Hanna said.

But Luna shook her head. "Chad Garber isn't interested in moving my furniture."

The man in question chose that moment to lift his head and meet Luna's gaze. A slow smile claimed his lips, and his eyes seemed to sparkle.

Dammit. Luna gritted her teeth. It was the same warm look

that had made her fall in love with him three years ago. The one that had broken her heart because she knew he'd never feel the same way about her. Not when he was an accomplished twenty-something professional pianist who was just being nice to the messed up seventeen-year-old foster kid that lived a few houses down. Still, she'd gotten over the broken heart, but what she couldn't handle was the fact that he knew her past—a past she'd left behind three years ago and had no intention of revisiting.

"Looks like he's interested in something," Shannon said, still eyeing Chad. "That look he's giving you is speaking volumes, Luna girl."

Hanna chuckled. "It sure is… and oh, here he comes."

Luna grabbed her latte and scone as she stood. "I should probably get to work. I don't want to be late."

"You still have plenty of time," Hanna said, glancing at the clock on the wall.

She was right, and since Luna was in the café almost every morning before she went to work, Hanna would certainly be aware of Luna's schedule. She opened her mouth to make an excuse about needing to get in for an early appointment, but before she had a chance, Chad arrived.

"Good morning, ladies," Chad said, his gaze lingering on Luna. "Did I hear something about someone needing a truck?"

"No. We were just—" Luna started.

"Yes," Shannon said, giving him one of her slow, seductive smiles. It was the kind designed to get men to do whatever she wanted them to do. Luna was torn between jealousy and amusement. The fact was Luna thought of Chad as hers, even if all he'd ever been was a concerned neighbor. Shannon placed a hand on Chad's arm and continued, "Luna needs someone to help her move her stuff into Hanna's house. She's finally moving from her temporary apartment in Eureka to Keating Hollow. That commute is killing her. And since you have a truck, plenty of muscles, and you're available most days, you seem like the obvious choice."

"Is that right?" he asked with a chuckle. "What makes you think I'm free?"

Shannon gave him a flat stare. "Come on, Chad. We all know you're still working on convincing Miss Maple to let you rent the store space next to A Spoonful of Magic. You can't do much with that new store of yours until you secure the space. Besides, you're here or at the Townsend brewpub almost every day. Maybe it's time to work off those five pounds you've packed on since you rolled into town a few months ago."

Chad glanced down at his flat abs for a moment and then raised one eyebrow. "Have you been checking me out, Shannon?"

She laughed. "Who hasn't?"

That was quite enough. Luna held up a hand. "Shannon, stop badgering Chad. I've got the move covered. Thanks for the breakfast, Hanna." She nodded to her friend and then waved at Shannon. "I'll see you later." Her eyes met Chad's troubled ones, and she nearly grimaced. She knew she was acting like a freak around him, but she just couldn't seem to get herself together. He brought back way too many memories she'd buried long ago. She forced herself to meet his blue gaze and gave him a fake smile as she said, "It was nice to see you again, Chad."

"You, too, Luna," he said quietly.

She paused for just a moment, staring at him. Then before anyone could say anything else, she mouthed, *Thank you.* He gave her a slight nod, and she took off, rushing out of the café.

Her head swam, and her pulse rate was so fast she wondered if she'd pass out.

"Snap out of it, Luna," she whispered to herself once she was standing out on the sidewalk of the storybook town. Behind her, the window display had been spelled with a scene of floating heart-shaped cookies that spelled out *Welcome to Keating Hollow*. A latte sat below the hearts, and the espresso art in the cup kept morphing into different shapes.

It was late May in Keating Hollow, and everything was blooming. Flowers filled planter boxes up and down both sides of the streets while the sun warmed Luna's chilled skin. She should have been ecstatic. She had a great job, new friends, a nice house to move into, and life was better than ever. Or at least it had been before Chad walked back into it.

She let out a huge sigh.

"What's wrong, Hope—er, I mean Luna?" the familiar, gruff voice was low and right behind her.

"You know what's wrong, Chad," she said, not even bothering to turn around. His presence had come as no surprise. In fact, she'd expected him to follow her out of Hanna and Rhys's engagement party the week before, and when he hadn't, even though she'd been thoroughly shaken, she had to admit she'd been disappointed.

He gently wrapped his left hand around hers and pulled her so that she was facing him. His brows were drawn together in confusion as his eyes searched hers. "No. I don't. You're obviously stressed about seeing me, but I don't know why. What did I do?"

"Nothing," she said quickly and stared down at their linked hands. Luna knew she should tug her hand out of his. It felt too good, and her heart had sped up while butterflies took over her stomach. What was wrong with her? She hadn't seen him in three years and even back then, they hadn't been an item. Chad was at least ten years her senior and far too honorable to consider hooking up with the messed-up foster kid that lived down the street.

"Well, that's good to know." Chad squeezed her hand and let go. His lips curled up into a small smile as he added, "Then there's no reason for me to not help you move your stuff into your new place. Just tell me where and when."

She couldn't help but chuckle. "You always were a sucker for playing the hero."

He let out a snort. "Maybe. But one thing's for sure, Luna Scott. The girl I knew back then was never helpless."

His words took her by surprise, and she couldn't help but grin. "That's the god's honest truth."

"But that doesn't mean she couldn't use the truck and muscle of an out-of-work musician to help her move a few things. How about tomorrow?"

She just stared at him, unsure of what to say. She couldn't avoid him forever in the small magical town, but that didn't mean it was smart to befriend him again. Her insides were already doing the jig. Bad idea. "I don't think—"

Chad shook his head. "Stop thinking, Luna. How about you just let an old acquaintance help you out? Think of it as the start of an apology for what went down back in Berkeley that last night we saw each other."

She scoffed. "What do you have to apologize for? I'm the one who ended up in juvy."

He winced. "I know, and it's all my fault."

7

CHAPTER 2

*H*ope... err, Luna blinked at him. Damn. Was he ever going to get used to calling her by her new name? He'd known her all these years as Hope, *his Hope*, and making that shift in his mind was proving to be all but impossible.

Her expression changed to pure skepticism as she scoffed, sounding just like the defiant, proud seventeen-year-old he'd known three years ago. "Please, Chad. Lose the guilty conscience. I don't need that on top of everything else. You had nothing to do with my arrest."

Before he could even respond, she turned on her heel and strode down the sidewalk with her head bent and shoulders hunched.

"Luna, wait!" he called and ran after her.

She let out a small sigh but didn't say anything as he fell into step beside her.

"I don't think you understand," he started.

"What's to understand? You feel guilty because you couldn't

save me. I get it." She paused and stared him right in the eye, hers blazing with a fierceness he'd seen more times than he could count. "But I don't need your pity. I never did."

"I don't pity you," he said automatically, and no truer words had ever been spoken. He'd hated her lot in life, the cards she'd been dealt. And all he'd ever wanted to do was lend her a hand up. Instead, he'd made a critical error, and as a direct result, she'd ended up spending time behind bars. "I admire the hell out of you, Luna. The strength you have... gods above. You have it in spades and always have. It's no surprise you made it through hell and came out the other side without any visible scars."

"I have scars, Chad," she said, looking past him, her eyes unfocused as if she were lost in her memories.

"I'm sure that's true. It doesn't change the fact that I think you're quite possibly the strongest person I've ever known."

She barked out a humorless laugh and crossed her arms over her chest, holding on tight as if staving off a chill. "Me? Strong? I just did what I had to do."

"I know," he said quietly, hating the haunted look on her face. He reached out and took her hand again, closing his fingers around hers. "Do you have a minute? There are a few things I'd like to clear up."

Luna closed her eyes and shook her head. "I have to get to work, and besides, I put my past behind me a long time ago, Chad. I don't want to talk about it. I'd appreciate it if you'd just let it go, too. Please."

What could he say to that? Nothing. She was practically pleading with him to let her move on. If that was what she needed in the moment, he'd keep his mouth shut. What other choice did he have, especially when she was on her way to work? "Of course, Luna. Anything you want."

She let out a breath she must've been holding, and her big green eyes bored into his as she said, "Thank you. I appreciate that."

"No need to thank me," he said, still not letting go of her hand. For some reason, he wanted to tug her into his arms and hold on for as long as she'd let him. Whoa. He took a half step back. *Where had that come from?*

She closed the distance and leaned in, her voice hushed as she asked, "Chad, can you do something for me?"

It was his turn to cross his arms over his chest, making sure he kept his hands to himself. Touching her was off limits. Wasn't it? A voice in the back of his head whispered she was a grown woman now. Why couldn't he hug her? He gave himself a mental shake, trying to dislodge the thoughts. He dug his fingers into his arms and said, "Sure. Anything."

"Nobody here knows about my past. And I'd like to keep it that way." She visibly swallowed and then continued, "I've worked hard to move past all of that. I don't want my boss and the rest of the town gossiping about me. Would you mind keeping the events of that time to yourself?"

He almost let out his own humorless bark of laughter. The last thing he wanted to do was talk about their shared past with anyone. He gave her a gentle smile before turning serious. "There's no need to worry. I have no intention of revisiting our time in Berkeley with the residents of this town. That's your story to tell when and if you want to. Not mine."

She dragged her intense gaze away and stared over his shoulder. "Thank you."

"There's no need for thanks. You know I'd never betray your trust like that."

Her lips curved up into the tiniest ghost of a smile. "You haven't changed."

This time he did laugh, thankful he didn't hear any bitterness in his chuckle. Weeks ago, he might have. "I think that remains to be seen, but hopefully I'm still the same guy you met on that stoop years ago." He winked at her. "And since you seemed to trust that guy okay, why don't you let me help you move your stuff? I'm happy to, you know. And Shannon is right. Until I get a lease on a music space, I don't have a lot to fill my time."

She hesitated.

Chad stared down at her, wishing with everything he had that she'd say yes. It wasn't that he was excited about moving furniture, especially with his messed-up hand. He just wanted to do whatever he could to make up for past mistakes. One day he'd tell her his part in that awful night when she went to jail, but not until she was ready to hear it. In the meantime, he was determined to be her friend. "Come on, Luna. My air magic will make it a heck of a lot easier on you. Not to mention, I already own a truck. You don't have to do everything on your own, you know."

Her smile vanished, and he wanted to kick himself. That had been the exact wrong thing to say, and Chad should've known better. If there was ever a human who was determined to not rely on anyone, it was Hope 'Luna' Scott. He cleared his throat. "I just meant you have free labor at your disposal. You'd be crazy to turn that down, right?"

She stared at her feet for a moment, and when she lifted her head, her expression had finally softened. "Your air magic and truck would come in quite handy."

He felt his shoulders relax as he gave her a little smile. "Ah-ha. That sounds suspiciously like a yes."

She chuckled. "You're awfully excited to move some furniture, Chad. I think maybe you need to get out more." Her eyes sparkled with mischief as she added, "Sign up for a dating app or two and get out there before you turn into an old spinster."

Why do I want a dating app when the most beautiful woman I've ever seen is standing right in front of me? Oh hell. He wasn't going there. She was a kid. Or she had been when he'd known her. She had to be twenty or twenty-one now. All grown up with a fulltime job and moving into her own place. *Snap out of it, Garber,* he ordered himself. Luna Scott was off limits. "What makes you think I'm not dating anyone?" he asked, trying to sound casual.

Her eyebrows shot straight up. "Oh? You have a girlfriend?"

"No," he admitted with a shrug. "I just wondered why you were so convinced I had no prospects."

She laughed again. "Please. In this town? If you had taken someone out, we all would have heard about it. The gossip runs through this town like river rapids." It was her turn to wink. "Okay, Mr. Helpful. Tomorrow at nine? Pick me up at the café, and we'll go move some furniture."

"Nine," he repeated with a nod and grinned at her before he walked off, determined to secure that music store lease.

"WELL HELLO THERE, CHAD," Miss Maple said, leading him into her office. She pushed a lock of her curly gray hair out of her eyes and removed her apron, revealing a flowy peasant blouse and skirt that looked like they were vintage early-seventies.

"What's this?" he asked as she handed him a paper cup. He took a sip and let out a small moan of pleasure as the rich chocolate hit his tongue.

"Salted caramel hot chocolate. Sounds like it's a winner." She sat down in her plush office chair and leaned back.

"Absolutely. That's better than..." His face heated as he swallowed his words. Talking about sex in any capacity with Miss Maple seemed inappropriate.

"Better than a poke in the eye?" she asked, her eyes glinting in the sunlight streaming through the window.

"Sure." Chad chuckled and placed the cup on the edge of her desk, leaning in. "I'm ready to make a deal on the retail space next door."

She raised one perfectly waxed eyebrow. "You are? Does that mean you're amenable to the two-year contract?"

"Yep. I'm in. Just as soon as the contract is ready, I'll be by to sign it," Chad said. When he'd previously spoken to Miss Maple, he'd requested a one-year contract. But she'd said she was only willing to rent the space to someone who intended to put roots down in the community. She'd already gone through two out-of-town tenants in the last three years who'd fallen in love with the quaintness of Keating Hollow but hadn't been ready to really invest in the community. Frankly, she was tired of the revolving door and the frustration of the townspeople when they saw another business close due to half-hearted attempts to fill a need within Keating Hollow.

Miss Maple clapped her hands together. "Excellent." With a smile claiming her lips, she opened a drawer and pulled out a file, handing it to him. "I knew you'd come around to my way of seeing things."

Chad chuckled and shook his head. "You were that sure, huh?"

"Sometimes I just get a feeling about people." She sat back and waited for him to read the contract.

When he was done, he glanced up. "There's no first and last

month's rent listed. Or a security deposit." He pushed the file back to her. "Add those in and I'll sign today."

She pushed the file back to him. "You're taking on a two-year lease. This is me meeting you halfway. Besides, I know how to track you down," she said with a teasing smile.

He snorted. Considering his stepmother lived in town and was his only remaining relative, she had a point. He whipped out his pen, signed, dated, and slid the contract back to her. "Thank you."

She reached across the desk and clasped her hand over his. "You're welcome." After making a copy of the lease, she handed Chad the paperwork and the keys.

Chad pocketed the keys and felt a bit of weight lift off his heart. Ever since the day he'd broken his hand, he'd felt rudderless and completely gutted by the consequences his stupidity had rained down on him. But now, he had a purpose and something to bring to the community that had saved him once before when he'd needed it most. He gave the older woman a grateful smile as he reached for the door knob. "I'll see you soon."

"Chad?" Miss Maple said, stopping him.

"Yeah?"

"I know you've found yourself here in Keating Hollow because of an unfortunate circumstance."

Unfortunate circumstance. He almost laughed at the characterization. If that's what she wanted to call beating the crap out of the biggest jackass he'd ever met, then sure. He could go with her version.

"I just think you should know we want you here, and Keating Hollow needs you," she said, her expression earnest. "Luna, in particular, needs you."

Her words stabbed him right in the heart, and he felt

himself retreating to that dark place that could swallow him whole for days on end. He wanted to argue with Miss Maple. Tell her in no uncertain terms that she was wrong. Instead, he just said, "Thanks for the retail space." Without another word, he left her office, silently closing the door behind him.

CHAPTER 3

*L*una ordered a large caramel latte, a skinny mocha, and two chocolate croissants as she tried to ignore the nerves jumping in her stomach. *Calm down,* she told herself. It wasn't as if this were a date with Chad. He was just going to help her move her stuff. Nothing more, nothing less.

That's a lie. She wanted to demand that the voice in her head shut its trap, but she knew that was futile. Her inner conscience had a big mouth.

"Happy moving day," Hanna said cheerily. "I bet you're looking forward to giving up that commute every day."

Luna smiled at her. "You've got that right. I might even get a bike and pedal myself to work on the sunny days now that the weather has turned nice."

Hanna glanced out the front window. "That's a good idea. Just know that the weather turns quickly around here sometimes. Especially in the spring. It will be sunny and warm and then a half hour later the storm clouds roll in off the ocean, and it can get ugly fast."

"Really? So far I've just seen some mist and light rain," Luna said, peering out at the clear, sunny sky.

"That's what makes it tricky." She gave Luna a smile and then nodded toward the front door. "Have fun today."

Luna turned and spotted Chad strolling through the door. His lips curved into a quiet smile.

"Morning," he said, his blue eyes scanning her.

She glanced down at her worn skinny jeans and faded secondhand T-shirt and shrugged. "Moving day clothes."

He lifted his gaze and let out a small bark of laughter. "You look more like you just stepped off the cover of *Rolling Stone*. Nice boots."

"Um, thanks." She felt her cheeks heat with embarrassment as butterflies fluttered in her gut. Was he flirting with her? He was. She was sure of it. And though she knew letting him get under her skin was a terrible idea, she couldn't help but enjoy his attention. She glanced down at her black, lace-up motorcycle boots. They weren't exactly her first choice for moving furniture, but the sole on one of her sneakers had come apart the night before. It was either her boots or sandals. The boots were safer.

He chuckled. "Come on, Luna. Let's go get you moved." He waved at Hanna.

"Wait. Breakfast," Hanna said, pushing the coffees and bag of croissants toward them.

"Thanks. That's kind of you," he said.

"Luna ordered it." Hanna's eyes sparkled with mischief as she winked at Luna.

With Chad behind her, Luna made a face at Hanna and mouthed *behave*.

Hanna's grin widened. "Have a good day, you two."

Luna picked up the bag and the cup with his name on it.

After she handed it to him, he took a sip and eyed Luna with a raised eyebrow. "You remembered."

"You ordered it the same way for over a year. I figured it was a safe bet," she said, berating herself for feeling self-conscious about remembering a detail about him.

"It definitely was." He pressed his hand to the small of her back as they walked out of the café.

Luna closed her eyes, hating how much she liked the way his hand felt. Dammit. She was not supposed to be going moony over this guy. He was about ten years older than her. Surely he didn't see her as anything more than just a younger-sister type. Or, more likely, she was just someone who always needed his help. And she hated that.

"Hop in," Chad said, opening the passenger door of his truck.

"Thanks." She climbed into the seat and moments later, they were rolling down the road, headed out of Keating Hollow. "Croissant?" she asked.

"Sure." They were silent as they passed groves of redwoods and nibbled on chocolate croissants. The traffic was light since it was later in the morning and a weekday, and Luna started to feel like they were the only two people out on the highway. It was disconcerting because her new life seemed to melt away, and her palms grew sweaty as she tried not to stare at the handsome man beside her. Suddenly she was seventeen again and in awe of the gorgeous man who'd never been anything but kind to her.

"So," Chad said, glancing over at her. "Catch me up on your life since we last saw each other."

Luna's stomach rolled with unease, and she glanced away, squeezing her eyes shut, trying to dispel the flashbacks of a time she'd never wanted to remember or talk about to anyone, let alone Chad.

"Luna?" he asked, concern evident in his tone. "I didn't mean to upset you."

Dammit. She let out a sigh, hating that she was showing any kind of weakness. "I'm not upset," she said, now gazing at the river that snaked along the side of the highway. "It's just weird to talk about. Most people don't know my past."

"Right." The truck rumbled down the road another couple of miles before he added, "You can talk to me, you know. I'd never judge you or betray your trust."

"I don't—" she started.

"Or you don't have to talk to me at all," he said, cutting her off. "I get it. Have you ever heard me talk about my past?"

That got her attention, and she turned to study his face. His expression was grim, but his lips were set in a determined line. "No. Never. All I ever knew about you is that you were some sort of piano prodigy and you spent some time in Keating Hollow as a kid before you were accepted into a performing arts school."

"You remembered that part about Keating Hollow?" he asked.

Her face heated, and she wondered if he suspected that part of the reason she'd ended up in the small town was because of him. It wasn't as if she'd expected to run into him. Last she'd heard, he'd still been traveling the world to play concerts and had even been laying down tracks for some recording artists. She hadn't actually expected him to ever show back up in the small town unless he happened to be visiting his stepmom. It was a big stretch to think she'd actually run into him.

No. Hoping to run into him hadn't been the plan at all. But he'd talked about the community of Keating Hollow with such fond memories, she'd already felt like she knew the place. Not to mention she had other reasons for heading north. Not least among them was the fact there had been an opening at a new spa, and when she spotted the ad, she'd jumped on the opportunity.

"Yeah," she said quietly. "You always made it sound like a magical place."

He laughed, his eyes full of amusement.

She replayed back her words in her mind. With an embarrassed chuckle of her own, she said, "I guess that's obvious and a major understatement. I just meant that the town sounded like heaven compared to the city. And when I saw the ad for the spa on a job site I was following, it was a no-brainer to apply. I was tired of the concrete jungle and fast pace of the city. Plus, I'd been commuting from the north bay up to Eureka before I got my apartment there a few times a month to work with Healer Snow. That lasted for about a year. I was tired of that drive."

"Sounds like it was the perfect situation for you," he said.

"I guess so." *Until you showed up,* she added silently. But even as the words rolled through her mind, they didn't exactly feel as true as they had the first time she'd run into him at Rhys and Hanna's engagement party. She'd been terrified of the town finding out she had a record and, if she was honest, afraid of being forced to face her own past. But now... He was just as easy to talk to as he had been three years ago.

"Tell me about the work you do with the healer." His eyes were on the road, paying attention to a particularly curvy section, and she was glad he wasn't looking at her when she spoke her next words.

"Um, you know I'm an earth witch, right?" she asked.

He nodded, still maintaining focus on the road.

She cleared her throat. "It turns out I'm skilled at helping the human body heal itself. So Healer Snow asked if I'd be willing to participate in some experiments with her, and now I'm helping her administer breakthrough treatments that honestly are life-saving. It's been... incredible, really."

Chad shot her a glance of pure awe, but then quickly focused on the road again. He didn't say anything, and Luna's palms got even sweatier. How come he wasn't asking questions? Everyone always did, and even though she rarely knew how to answer them, she knew that what she did was rare and special, causing intense curiosity. But Chad was just driving along as if she'd told him that she was Healer Snow's coffee girl.

Just as Luna was about to let out a huff of irritation, the truck swerved off the road into a lookout area over the river. Chad slammed the gearshift into park and turned to face her. His gaze was intense when he asked, "You have a gift so powerful that you're helping Healer Snow save lives?"

A nervous giggle bubbled up from the back of her throat. "Um, I wouldn't exactly put it that way, but yes. What I do has helped cure rare conditions and isolate problematic genes."

"Put it what way?" he asked, appearing genuinely confused. "That you're powerful or that you save lives?"

As usual, he'd just called her out on her modesty when it came to her gifts. For as long as she could remember, Chad had been the only person during her formative years to see her as someone worthy of praise. Now Healer Snow and her clients at A Touch of Magic clearly showed appreciation, but that was different. They didn't know the real her. The one she hid away from everyone because she just knew they'd find out she wasn't worthy. Luna shook her head and scolded herself for succumbing to those destructive thoughts... again. Logically, she knew that she was worthy of love, respect, and friendship. It was just that her heart didn't agree. It had grown a shield, and she was not at all interested in letting anyone have a piece of it again.

"That I'm powerful," she said with a shrug. "I don't think I'm any more gifted than any other witch."

He snorted. "Okay. If you say so."

She knew that tone. He clearly didn't agree with her assessment but was willing to let it go. It was one of the things she liked about him most. He didn't hide what he was thinking, but he also didn't feel it was necessary to argue just to be right.

Chad put the truck back in gear and pulled onto the road. "How did you find out you had the ability to heal people?"

She'd known the question was coming, and even though she never talked about how she'd discovered her gift, this time she found herself wanting to tell him. She wanted him to know that she'd stayed strong through everything, and even though her life had been crap, it hadn't broken her. "My first clue was when I was in juvy."

Her words hung in the air as she waited for him to say something, anything. But when he just gave a tiny nod of encouragement, she let out a breath, feeling the ache in her chest loosen. "My bunkmate was jumped one night. She was bleeding and needed stitches, but the guard on duty for our section wasn't a good guy. If she went to him, who knows what would've happened to her."

Chad sucked in a sharp breath and glanced at her with haunted eyes.

She turned away, hating the horror and pity she saw there. Luna had accepted her role in the crime that had landed her butt in jail a long time ago. If he was going to be a friend now, he'd have to accept it, too. But it wasn't up to her to help him through it. "Anyway, I was cleaning a cut over her eye as best I could when my magic just flared to life as if I didn't have any control over it. Her cut healed enough that it stopped bleeding. I even managed to soothe the bruise on her jaw so that it didn't ache anymore."

"That's incredible, Ho—I mean Luna," he said and shot her an apologetic smile. "Sorry. I'm trying to get it right."

She returned his smile with a tiny one of her own. "I know. It's okay."

Relief flashed in his blue eyes. "That's pretty incredible. It sounds like your gift jumped out when you needed it most. What happened after that?"

Luna wasn't sure she wanted to travel all the way down memory lane. There were far too many potholes down that path. So she skipped all the drama and said, "There was a re-entry counselor who learned what I could do and advised me to seek out an education as a healer." Luna snorted. "Can you imagine being in juvy with no family, no friends, no money, no anything to fall back on and trying to figure out not only how you're going to take care of yourself once you get out, but how to even get into college, let alone pay for it?"

"No," he said quietly and steered the truck onto Highway 1 South, toward her temporary apartment. "I can't imagine how impossible that must've seemed."

"Exactly. Anyway, college wasn't happening. I had no idea what I was going to do other than get a job and stay the hell away from my foster mom and her shady boyfriend."

"What did you do?" he asked. "How did you end up a massage therapist?"

"Oh. That. I got as far from Berkeley as I could reasonably go on limited resources. Eventually I found a room to rent with a bunch of college students, and got a job at a coffee shop.

I had experience and could work the morning shift. The manager was so desperate she hired me on the spot without even asking for references." She shrugged. "It was a decent job. My manager's brother came in every morning on his way to massage therapy school, and eventually I decided that was as good a gig as any and a heck of a lot cheaper than trying to go to college. So as soon as I had the funds, I enrolled. It was while I was there that I met Healer Snow. She was a guest lecturer. One of my instructors told her about my ability, and she sought me out. The rest is history."

Chad didn't say a word. He just reached over and slipped his hand over hers, squeezing lightly. The gesture startled her at first, but then his skin was so warm, so foreign, but also just... right, that she squeezed back, grateful for the human connection she rarely experienced. Sure, she touched people for a living, but no one touched *her*, and his hand, wrapped around hers, almost brought tears to her eyes. She held them back, and without conscious thought she stroked her thumb over the back of his hand and froze when she sensed more than felt the pain radiating beneath the surface of his skin.

"Chad?" she asked.

"Yeah?"

She squeezed his hand gently. "Is this why you're in Keating Hollow?"

He nodded and took a deep breath. "My piano career is over."

CHAPTER 4

*C*had was honestly surprised Luna hadn't heard about his fall from superstar pianist to has-been musician. She'd been right when she'd mentioned the gossip mill in Keating Hollow. It wasn't a secret that his career was over or that it was the reason he'd ended up in the small town with the intent to open a music store. If he couldn't play at an elite level anymore, he could at least teach and provide a venue for other people to explore their musical whims. "It's not the end of the world. Just an adjustment."

Luna let out a humorless laugh. Her tone turned quiet as she said, "Maybe not the end of the world, but it's certainly grave enough that anyone in your shoes would be shaken, Chad."

Shaken was a good word, he decided. It described his state of being in more ways than one. He'd ruined his hand and his career when he'd lost his cool during that altercation. Chad knew he'd been hot-headed. Hasty. Stupid as hell. But as he glanced over at Luna and saw a glimpse of her seventeen-year-old self as she caught her bottom lip between her teeth, he knew he wouldn't change a thing. If Leo Mahoney ever stepped into Luna's or his path again, he'd be more than happy to use the guy's face as a punching bag… without a single regret.

"I'm sorry," Luna said, glancing away. "I'm sure that's not something you want to talk about."

Chad flexed his fingers, trying to stretch through the ache in his hand. "You have nothing to be sorry for. It was difficult right after I realized I'd thrown away my career. But I've accepted it. To tell you the truth, I'm kind of glad to be settling down in one place after all these years. Being on the road all the time doesn't exactly make it easy to form relationships."

Luna raised her eyebrows at him. "Are you saying you don't have a girlfriend or anyone special in your life?"

He snorted. "Being on the road is lonely. Not only do I not have a girlfriend, the truth is I don't even really have any friends, unless you count my manager and my agent. Which I do. But I'd really like to know what it's like to have people in my life that aren't there just to make money off me. You know?"

She gave a tiny shake of her head, and he realized what a stupid idea that was, expecting her to relate to the pressures of touring. That life was glamorous right up until the realities sank in. He loved playing the piano, but his life had become a series of broken connections. He was hoping settling in Keating Hollow would change that.

"My money problems have always had to do with not having enough," she said with a nervous chuckle. "Call me crazy, but I think it might be nice to try the opposite problem for a while."

He gave her a knowing smile. "Yeah. Fair enough."

A comfortable silence fell between them for the rest of the

ride to her shabby apartment in Eureka. Just as he put the truck into park, Luna turned to him and said, "Hey. You didn't tell me what happened to your hand. Were you in some kind of accident?"

He turned and met her brilliant green eyes and knew he should just come out and say it. This was his chance to come clean. She deserved to know. "I was provoked and—"

Knock, knock, knock.

The loud rapping came from the driver's side window, and Chad jumped, startled by the noise. "Holy crows," he whispered, lowering the window to the young, skinny teenager who'd stepped back from the truck, glancing around like he was panicked someone might see him.

Luna chuckled. "Holy crows? You sound like an old man."

"I feel like it after that major heart attack." He sucked in a breath and turned to the teen, noting his jeans were frayed and his cheeks had the hollow look of a person who routinely didn't have enough to eat. "What can I help you with, man?" he asked, keeping his voice friendly. The last thing he wanted to do was scare the kid off.

"Um." The teen stared straight into Chad's eyes, his expression determined. "I was wondering if you needed any help with anything. If I could run a few errands for some cash. I could wash your truck or clean your apartment." His gaze flickered away, and he forced out, "Or anything else you might be willing to pay a few bucks for."

Unfiltered rage filled Chad's chest as he realized what the kid was implying. He wanted to yell at him, climb out of the truck, and shake him for even suggesting such a thing, but he knew his anger was misplaced. The kid was obviously living on the streets and just trying to survive. "Sure, kid. You're in luck, actually. Luna here is moving today, so we could use a hand carrying her stuff to the truck. You up for that?"

The kid's dark brown eyes lit up, and he nodded enthusiastically.

"How much for a couple hours of your time?" Chad asked.

"Just, um, whatever you can spare."

Chad nodded. "All right. How's twenty an hour sound?"

The young man's mouth hung open for just a second. "Yeah. I mean, yes. That sounds good."

"Let's get to work then." Chad climbed out of the truck and held his hand out. "I'm Chad Garber, and this is Luna Scott." He waved to her. "And you are?"

The boy hesitated as his gaze flickered back and forth between Luna and Chad. After taking a deep breath and shaking Chad's hand, he said, "Levi."

"It's nice to meet you, Levi," Chad said.

Luna moved forward, her expression curiously neutral as she took a turn to shake the young man's hand. "I'm going to grab some breakfast sandwiches before we start. Do you prefer bacon or sausage?"

His eyes widened before filling with longing. But instead of answering her question, he said, "You don't have to do that. I'm fine."

The hungry look on his face betrayed his words, and Luna said, "Well, I'll get you something anyway in case you change your mind. Moving furniture is appetite-inducing work."

She kept her tone light, but Chad could see that her heart was breaking for the kid. As far as he knew, Luna had never been homeless, but her situation had been precarious enough that it had always been a possibility. Her foster mother was a real piece of work.

"Here." Luna handed Chad a single door key. "It's apartment 12. Upstairs. I'll be right back."

As she started walking across the parking lot toward a fast food restaurant, Levi called out, "Bacon."

"Got it," she said without even turning around.

"Well, looks like it's time to get started, Levi," Chad said, jerking his head toward the stairs that led to Luna's apartment. "Ready to show me what you've got?"

The kid gave him a shaky smile and nodded.

"Good deal. Let's see what we've got to move." Chad led the way and totally forgot that before Levi interrupted him, he was about to spill his guts to Luna.

CHAPTER 5

That all-encompassing fear that Luna had lived with for the majority of her adolescence came slamming back into her the moment she'd realized that Levi was just a hungry, scared kid, trying to earn a bit of money without having to sell himself. She couldn't imagine what his life must be like, but it was obvious he needed food. He had that malnourished look that made him appear to be disappearing right before your eyes.

All she wanted to do was wrap her arms around him and tell him he was safe now. But he wasn't, and no amount of her wishing he was would change his reality. Not today anyway. But she could feed him. Granted, fast food wasn't the best option, but it was close and fit her own modest budget.

After purchasing enough food for five, Luna jogged back to her apartment and found Chad and Levi packing up her dishes. She set the bags on the counter and said, "You don't have to do that. I'll tackle that while you guys start loading the truck."

Chad and Levi both shook their heads. Chad glanced at

him and chuckled. "Looks like this isn't Levi's first moving rodeo."

Levi's face was dark and brooding before he turned his back to them and concentrated on packing her plates. Luna knew that look. It was the same one she'd worn when something pushed all her buttons. She had no doubt that Levi had moved more times than he could count. And she wondered if his parents had finally lost the housing battle and that's why he was on the streets or if he'd been forced out for some reason. Whatever the cause for his situation, she wasn't really in a position to help, but her heart ached to, and her head screamed that she couldn't just walk away from this kid once her stuff was loaded in the truck. But she knew better than anyone that no matter how much she wanted to help, there was a better-than-decent chance the kid wouldn't accept what little she had to offer. He'd likely be too suspicious. She had been. It had taken Chad months to break down her barriers and get her to trust him. One day of food and a promise of forty bucks was likely to be the best they could do for him.

"Okay, why won't you let me pack my own kitchen?" Luna asked, confused.

Chad chuckled. "You might want to take care of the bedroom."

Luna frowned, knowing all she had were some clothes and some toiletries. Nothing big. But then she stepped into the bedroom and groaned. She'd completely forgotten she'd hung up most of her unmentionables three days earlier. She'd actually been staying in the house in Keating Hollow, using an air mattress for sleeping because she hadn't wanted to make the drive. Now Chad and Levi knew she wore a lot of matching black lace undergarments. The skimpy kind, because they made her feel bold and powerful when she otherwise just felt exhausted.

With her head held high, Luna returned to the other room and started removing the food from the bags. "Eat first. Load later."

Levi's gaze landed on the paper-wrapped breakfast sandwiches and hash browns she'd set on a paper plate. He was frozen, his eyes fixated on the meal.

Without making a big deal out of it, she casually handed him the plate. "There's a soda there for you, too," she said, taking her own plate and sitting on the secondhand sofa. A moment later, Chad joined her. Neither looked back at Levi as they dug into the sandwiches.

Luna wasn't even hungry yet, but she choked the sandwich down, wanting to make damn sure that Levi didn't feel uncomfortable eating the meal she'd purchased for him. "There's more in the bag, Levi," she said. "Eat your fill. I know when I was your age, I was ravenous all the time." It was the truth. There was never enough to go around at her foster family's home.

"This is fine," he said.

Luna didn't push it. Whatever they had left after moving, she'd insist he take it. It might not be fresh, but it'd still be edible.

"Okay. Ready to get to work?" Chad said, rising from the sofa.

"Yep. I'll take care of the bedroom," Luna said, already over her embarrassment about her hanging underwear. Chad was a grown man. Surely he'd seen his share of woman's lingerie before. "Shouldn't take but just a few minutes, then I'll be out to help with the kitchen."

It took Luna less than ten minutes to pack up her clothes

and toiletries and to strip the bed. Once she was done, she joined the guys in the kitchen. "The bedroom is ready. If you two want to haul the bed to the truck, I'll finish up the dishes."

Levi carefully tucked a newspaper-wrapped mug in one of the boxes. "Most of the cabinets are already empty."

"Thanks." She smiled at him.

He rewarded her with a shy smile of his own, and Luna thought her heart was going to break right in two. The kid was sweet, not yet too hardened by whatever he was going through in his young life.

"Let's go, kid," Chad said. "I'll show you the wonders of my air magic."

"You're a witch?" he asked, his face lighting with interest.

"Sure. So is Luna, only her talents lie in earth magic."

"So cool." He glanced back and forth between them before dipping his head and adding, "I wish I knew what kind of witch I am."

Luna met Chad's gaze with her eyebrows raised in question. How could he not know? The elements were pretty straight forward. Chad shrugged one shoulder, indicating he was at a loss, too. "What do your parents think?" Luna asked tentatively.

It was Levi's turn to shrug. "I don't know. My mom is gone, and my dad isn't magical. He never wanted to hear anything about it. It's not his thing."

Gone. Did that mean his mother had passed? Just like Luna's adoptive mother. She felt her chest tighten and wanted to ask him a million questions, but she kept them to herself. Instead she said, "But you're pretty sure you're a witch? What makes you think so?"

Levi surprised her by letting out a bark of laughter. But he clamped his mouth shut and stared at his feet as he said, "I get premonitions. They always come true."

Luna sucked in a breath.

His head snapped up. "What? You think I'm a freak, too? I thought witches would be more accepting of unusual abilities."

There was panic in his eyes now, and Luna rushed to reassure him. "No, no. Nothing like that. In fact, you're not a freak at all." She wanted to reach out and squeeze his hand, reassure him through her touch, but she could see he was ready to bolt. He was glancing between the leftover bag of food and the door. If he hadn't needed the money Chad had promised him, he probably would've grabbed the bag and fled. "Not a freak," she reiterated. "Special. Witches who are seers are called spirit witches, and they are rare."

His eyes went wide, and his face flushed. "I'm probably not..." He cleared his throat. "That's probably unlikely that I... I don't think I'm a spirit witch."

Luna hadn't witnessed his gift, so it wasn't as if she could refute his denial. Instead she said, "Time will tell. Are you ready to help Chad maneuver the furniture downstairs?"

"Sure."

The pair disappeared into the bedroom while Luna finished up the kitchen.

A couple hours later, most of Luna's meager possessions were packed into the bed of the truck with the rest shoved into the cab. Luna handed Levi the two leftover sandwiches while Chad pressed fifty dollars into his hand.

"Thanks for your help," Chad said.

His hand shook as he stared at the money clutched in his grip. He seemed to steal himself as he thrust it back toward Chad. "That's too much. I can't take this."

"You can," Chad said evenly. "I offered twenty dollars an hour. That was the agreement, and I'm a man of my word."

Luna watched him with tears stinging the backs of her eyes. She knew he was a good person, but here he was, proving it all over again.

"Keep the money, Levi," Chad said softly.

Levi gave him a tiny nod and shoved the bills into his front pocket. "Thank you," he said, his voice breaking slightly. He turned his head away, and that flush came roaring back.

"Levi?" Luna asked, slipping her arm through his thin one.

"Yeah?"

"Can I ask you something?" She knew she was on shaky ground, but she had to try.

"I guess so."

She walked him outside and sat on the top step of the stairs, indicating for him to join her.

He did but said nothing, just staring at the truck they'd just loaded with a wistful look on his face.

"Do you have somewhere safe to go after you leave here? A family that takes care of you?" Luna asked, praying for his sake that the answer was yes. But when he hesitated, she knew the answer. "Are you in foster care?"

He hung his head but stayed silent.

"I was in foster care for many years," she said, keeping her voice low and neutral. "It wasn't always a safe place to be."

His head snapped up, and he stared at her with those wide brown eyes. "What did you do when it wasn't safe?"

Luna glanced over at Chad but quickly looked away. He'd let her crash on his couch a few times, but mostly she'd taken refuge with schoolmates. "I had a couple of friends who didn't mind me crashing every once in a while. When that failed, I just tried to disappear in the city for a while and then would sneak back in thc house when I knew everyone was asleep."

Levi stood, still holding the fast food bag she'd insisted he take with him. "That sucks. But my situation isn't like yours."

"I'm sure it isn't. But if you need help, Chad and I are willing to do whatever we can to better your situation."

His eyes flashed with distrust. "You two aren't some sort of sicko kidnappers, preying on the weak, are you? Because otherwise, I don't see why you're trying to be so nice to some grungy kid you just met."

"Levi—" Luna started.

But before she could voice her protest, he spun on his heel and started to jog along the balcony toward another set of stairs.

"Damn," Luna muttered, pushing her hair back. "That did not go as I planned."

"At least he took the food bag with him," Chad said.

"That's only enough food for tonight," Luna said, feeling her ire rise. "What about tomorrow? Or the next day? Or when he's sick or getting himself assaulted for just existing. How is what we did today going to help him then?"

Chad gave her a slow smile. "That's where the business card and note comes in."

"What business card and note?" Luna asked, narrowing her eyes at him.

"The ones I put in the takeout bag. They are on top of the sandwiches. Once he digs in, he'll find them."

Luna watched as Levi reached the bottom of the stairs and disappeared around the side of the building. "What did the note say?"

Chad stepped up beside her. "I said that I was worried that he might not have a safe place to stay or enough for basic necessities and that if he needed anything, anything at all, that he should call you or me for help. My card has my personal cell number, and I hand wrote the spa's number."

Luna turned to look at him, her insides a jumble of emotions. Chad had always found nonthreatening ways to let her know he was someone she could count on when she needed someone. There was the time when her foster mother's boyfriend of the week had been getting a little handsy, and instead of confronting the asshat, knowing it would only make her living situation worse, Chad had offered her a job cleaning his house. Said he needed it done by the next morning. His offer was perfect. It had given her control over whether she wanted his help or not by accepting or declining to clean his house. She'd jumped on it. Anything was better than being mauled by the pervert boyfriend.

When she'd gotten to his residence, she didn't see a speck of dust in sight, but he'd still paid her to clean his small house, insisting it had been a few weeks since anyone had vacuumed. By the time she was done, he'd handed her enough money to foot her lunch bill for the next week and given her a weekly gig to keep the place in order. Two weeks later, she found out he had a regular housekeeper who showed up every Monday whether the house needed it or not. She never did tell him she knew his secret and ended up working for him until she'd been hauled off to juvy.

As the memories washed through her, Luna's eyes misted. And before she could stop herself, she flung her arms around him, buried her face into his shoulder, and said, "Thank you."

His arms came up and tentatively wrapped around her, pulling her in closer in a completely satisfying hug. "For what?" he whispered.

Luna tightened her grip on him and said, "For being you."

CHAPTER 6

C had pulled up in front of the sweet cream-colored cottage with red shutters and killed the engine. "Nice place. Looks like it's walking distance to Main Street."

Luna nodded. "It's just about perfect for me." She let out a quiet chuckle. "Actually, it's a lot more than I'm used to. I'm not sure why I need two bedrooms, but I'm looking forward to figuring it out. The largest place I've ever lived in on my own was that apartment we just left in Eureka."

"You deserve this, Luna," Chad said, reaching over and squeezing her hand. "I'm glad you made your way to Keating Hollow."

Her lips curved up into a ghost of a smile. "Me, too."

Chad was reluctant to let go of her hand and just sat there, enjoying her for a moment.

Eventually she raised her gaze to his and said, "We should probably unload the truck."

"Right." His voice was thick with emotion, and he had to shake himself. What the hell was going on with him? *Snap out of it, dude,* he told himself. *Don't go there. There's too much history, and some of it she doesn't even know about.*

Chad pulled his hand away and hopped out of the truck.

Luna climbed down and trotted up the pretty flower-lined walkway to unlock the door.

Chad chuckled to himself. No one in Keating Hollow locked their doors. No one but Luna Scott anyway. He knew why. She'd never lived in a place that was safe enough to trust the neighbors. And he was certain trust was never going to come easily for her.

They got to work, unloading the truck. When it came time to unload the bed, Luna leaned against the truck bed and sucked in a long breath. "It would've been really nice to have Levi here."

Chad nodded, flexing his aching hand. He was mentally fatigued from using his air magic and had fallen back on manual labor for most of the unloading. While the rest of his body was keeping up all right, his hand had curled into a slight claw, and he knew it'd be a few days before the pain eased.

"Are you okay?" Luna asked, eyeing his hand.

"I will be. Just needed a minute before we tackle this bed." He flexed again, trying to stretch the muscles and tendons, but a sharp pain ran up his arm and he winced.

Luna inched closer to him and gently took his hand in hers. "Do you mind if I try something?"

He stared into her green eyes, enjoying her gentle caress.

"Chad?"

"Yeah?"

She laughed. "Where'd you go?"

"Your touch. It just feels good on my achy joints."

"I can do better than that," she said, running all four of her fingers over the back of his. "Do you mind if I try something?"

42

"Not at all." He closed his eyes and then let out a contented sigh as magical tingles sparked off her fingertips and danced over his skin. A small moan of appreciation escaped his lips before he could rein himself in. "Damn. That's really nice."

"Just wait until I actually start trying," she said, her voice full of amusement.

"If this is you being half-assed in the magic department, your skills must be a damned miracle."

Her eyes sparkled at the praise, and he vowed to do everything he could to put that look on her face again. "Relax for me," she said, and her magic began pulsing with more intensity.

"I'm not sure that's possible." But he closed his eyes anyway, trying not to think about how her touch was making him want to grab her and fuse his lips to hers. He was lit up inside just from her running her fingertips over his hand.

"Take a deep breath," she soothed. "Picture yourself at the piano, playing that one song I always loved. The one that I told you sounded like sunshine and happiness."

The memory of her sitting at his piano in Berkeley as he tapped out the notes to a song his mother had written when he was a child warmed him inside. It was his favorite memory of her, one of the rare times when she'd seemed truly at peace.

"That's it," she said softly. "Perfect." She moved from caressing to lightly massaging his hand, pressing her strong fingers into his palm. The tension seemed to just melt away under her touch. But she didn't stop there. Once she'd worked over his palm, she moved on to each of his fingers, pressing and stretching and stimulating the muscles and tendons.

"You're amazing at this," Chad said, stifling another moan of pleasure.

"Thanks. You really should come in for regular massage

therapy visits. I think I can do a lot to help with your movement and flexibility."

"All right. Sure." His stomach did a little flip at the thought of seeing her on a regular basis. Only instead of trying to tamp down his affection for her like he'd been doing for the past few days, he just smiled at her. "I'll make an appointment later when I get home."

Luna spent a few more minutes massaging and treating his hand, and by the time she was done, he barely felt any traces of the ache that he'd been living with for over three months.

He flexed his fingers with ease and stared at her in wonder. "How did you do that? Nothing I've done with the physical therapist has even come close to what you managed in just a few minutes."

She gave him a shy smile. "My training helps, but it was mostly my earth magic. Restoring muscles, tendons, etcetera comes naturally to me. It's no big deal."

Chad stared at her intently. "It is a big deal, Luna. You must know what your gift can mean to people who have suffered a serious injury."

"I do." She glanced away. "It's just that I don't like to make a big deal out of it. I'm not a miracle worker, Chad. I just do what I can to help people."

Her words hit him straight in the gut. She was sweet, gorgeous, and had the biggest heart of anyone he'd ever met. It wasn't just impressive; it was a downright miracle. After the rough upbringing she'd had, it would be easy for her to be bitter. But she wasn't. She was truly kind and loving. The way she'd jumped right into action grabbing plenty of food when she realized Levi was an at-risk youth and then the way she was upset when he bolted had touched him. She cared about people and it showed. "You've grown into one hell of a woman, you know that?"

Her intense green eyes met his. "Is that right? I was certain you still saw me as that scared teen who was always hanging around."

"Well, I did." His lips turned up into a teasing grin, and his eyes sparked with humor. "But then I saw all that lace in your bedroom."

Luna groaned. "Don't remind me."

Laughing, he led the way to the back of the truck. "Come on, gorgeous. Let's get your bed into that cute house of yours so you have somewhere better than that air mattress to sleep tonight."

Once they hauled the bed up the stairs and got it put together, Luna stood in the middle of the master bedroom with her hands on her hips. "That's everything, right?"

"Yep. The truck is empty," Chad confirmed.

"Perfect." Luna walked over to him and held her hand out, waiting to shake his. "Thanks for the help today. It's much appreciated."

Chad slipped his hand into hers, but instead of shaking it, he pulled her in for an all-encompassing hug. "Handshakes are for acquaintances, Luna. Not old friends."

"Is that what we are?" she asked, her voice slightly muffled by his chest.

Pulling back, Chad glanced down at her lovely face. "Definitely."

"Yeah, okay." She pressed her face to his shoulder. And this time, she pulled him in, holding on so tight he almost had trouble breathing. Or was that because his heart was in his throat? This lovely creature was making all of his nerves dance. He had the simultaneous urges to both stay locked in the embrace forever, but to also pull back so that he could cup her face and kiss her senseless.

Damn. Kissing wasn't "old friends." And Chad knew if he dared cross that line after only one day of working together, she'd likely bolt. Or freeze him out. She hadn't signed up to be hit on. He needed to cool the hell off before he did something he'd regret.

"I should go," Chad said, forcing himself to step away from her. "I'm sure you want to get settled in and get some rest before work tomorrow."

Luna glanced at her phone, checking the time. "That's probably not a bad idea."

"Okay then." Chad started to move toward the bedroom door.

"Chad?" she called.

"Yeah?"

"Thank you." She gave him an appreciative smile, her eyes warm with gratitude. "I meant it when I said your help today was very much appreciated. Will you let me take you to dinner tomorrow night as a thank you?"

The words were out of his mouth before he even gave her invitation any thought. "Yes. Absolutely. Where and when?"

"Seven?" She bit her lower lip, drawing his gaze. "The Townsend brewpub?"

"Sure. Seven. The brewpub." He grinned at her, and right before he left, he added, "It's a date."

CHAPTER 7

*I*t's a date. The words rolled around in Luna's head as she worked on Ms. Betty's neck and shoulder area, gently massaging away a few knots. Ever since Chad had uttered the words just before leaving her house the day before, she'd been in a state of mild panic. Was that really what she'd done? Asked him out on a date?

No. It was just a thank-you dinner. Nothing else.

Then why was she stressing about what she was going to wear and wondering if she had time to get her nails done after work?

"Ahhhh," Ms. Betty said, moaning her appreciation. "I wish I would've known you forty years ago. This is better than sex with my late husband Gordy."

Luna blinked and looked down at her client. Chuckling she said, "That's… maybe a little TMI, Betty."

"I'm just speaking my truth," the older woman said. "I'm telling you, your hands are heavenly. Imagine if you used them on my—"

"Oh no. No imagining anything, and for the goddess's sake,

do not voice that thought or I will end this session before I get to the other shoulder."

"Buzzkill," Betty said, and Luna could almost hear the eye roll in the woman's voice.

"This is a professional environment, Ms. Betty." Luna tried to keep her voice stern but couldn't help the giggle of amusement that gave her away.

"Sure, like you've never peeked beneath the sheet when a hottie comes in for a rub down." The woman's body shook with her laughter. "Do you ever forget and let out a groan when you see a truly gorgeous ass?"

"There is no peeking. Please, I'm a pro." Luna poured more oil into her palm, enjoying the faint orange-ginger scent she'd chosen that morning.

"Uh-huh. Are you telling me you wouldn't sneak a glance at Chad's round tush if he booked a session with you?"

"Nope. Never," Luna insisted.

"What about after your date tonight?" she said, her voice high-pitched with excitement. "Do you have plans to peel him out of those tight jeans? I bet he has a stellar backside."

Luna stared down at the gray-haired woman and blinked. She took a deep breath, trying to calm her nerves. After moving to Ms. Betty's other shoulder, she asked, "How did you know we're... um, going to dinner tonight?"

"Oh, Luna, honey. This is a small town. Everyone knows everything."

Luna frowned. She hadn't mentioned her date with Chad to anyone. Had she? But then it dawned on her she'd told Hanna when she'd gone in for her morning coffee, but only because the other woman had invited her to a girls' night with the Townsend sisters. Luna had been disappointed she'd had to decline. She liked hanging with them. But she couldn't, nor did she want to, cancel on Chad. The truth was she was looking forward to seeing him. She was disappointed that Hanna was spreading her business, but then again, someone at the shop could've overheard the conversation. Betty was right. There weren't any secrets in the small town... except Luna's past. Chad was the only one who knew her secrets. Did she trust him to keep them? She thought so.

Another appreciative moan came from Ms. Betty. "By the time you're done, I'm gonna need someone to carry me back to the home."

Luna smirked. Ms. Betty lived in a senior citizen community on the outskirts of town. But she always made it sound like she'd checked into an assisted living situation, which couldn't be further from the truth. Ms. Betty was just as mobile and capable as the rest of the town's citizens.

"Do you have anyone on staff that can help with that? Hunter maybe? I wouldn't mind being wrapped in his muscular arms, let me tell you. Just pressing my face into his pecs would be enough to tide me over for weeks," she said in a breathy tone.

"Don't let Faith hear you talking about her man like that. She's a little on the jealous side sometimes," Luna said. "Wouldn't want to get in a cat fight right after the massage, would you?"

Betty let out a huff of laughter. "Faith doesn't have anything on me. I'm a brown belt, you know."

"You are?" Luna asked, surprised.

"Well, I have a brown belt. My first husband earned it. All I did was cheer him on. But I figure I must've learned something after all those years of pretending to be interested in karate. Right?"

"Sure, Betty." Luna chuckled. "I bet you have moves Faith's never seen before."

"You got that right." She wiggled her hips, making Luna laugh again.

"Looks more like dance moves."

"I've got those, too, Luna. You should come to our next dance social at the home. I'll show you my trick-hip move. Of course, I might need some physical therapy afterward, but it'd be worth it."

Betty continued to charm Luna with her stories through the rest of the massage, and when it was over and Luna walked her back to the front counter, they were both still laughing.

"Well now, what's got the two of you in stitches today?" Lena, the receptionist, asked. Her dark hair was piled on top of her head in a sleek bun, and she had a pencil tucked along her ear. Black-rimmed glasses topped off her aesthetic, making her look more like a Hispanic librarian than a spa receptionist.

"Nothing much," Ms. Betty said with a small shrug. "I was just hoping to run into Hunter." She lifted her hands and mimed squeezing his biceps. "I swear, that man does things to me. Last week I almost pinched his butt, but Yvette over at Hollow Books told me that's harassment, so I just tapped it instead. Do you have any idea how firm that thing is? I could just take a bite—"

"Ms. Betty!" Faith scolded as she swept into the lobby. Her long blond hair was pulled back into a low braid, and her green eyes were narrowed as she stared at the older woman. "You did not just brag about sexually harassing my fiancé, did you?"

"I didn't pinch him! Yvette said—"

Faith put her hand up, stopping the older woman. "I know what Yvette said. Copping a feel isn't any better." She shook her head. "How would you like it if I reached out and grabbed your butt?"

Ms. Betty's eyes flickered with amusement. "I'd say thank you. It would be the most action I've seen since that Y2K party where we pulled watches from a bucket and I ended up spending the evening with that gorgeous restaurateur from the city. He had a really big—"

"Never mind." Faith clamped her hands over her ears and shook with silent laughter.

Luna adored Ms. Betty. The woman had to be in her seventies and possessed no filter. While Luna didn't wish to offend anyone with inappropriate touching, she did hope that when she was Ms. Betty's age, she was embracing life as fully as the older woman did. Ms. Betty always had a smile on her face and never missed a chance to laugh. It was a sign of life well lived as far as Luna was concerned.

Ms. Betty settled her bill with Lena, and when she was on her way out, she squeezed Luna's hand as she said, "Enjoy that sexy man. Take notes. I'm gonna wanna hear all about it during my next session."

Luna let out a snort of amusement. "Have a good afternoon, Betty."

"You know it. The pool boy is coming by today. I need to get back before all the good seats are taken." With a giant smile, she hurried out the door, climbed onto the Enchanted Dreams Retirement Community golf cart, and waved as the young man in the driver's seat backed out.

"She's dangerous," Faith said under her breath.

"I think she's fun," Luna said with a shrug and started to head back to her massage space to get it ready for the next client.

"Wait, Luna there's a letter for you," Faith said.

Luna glanced back at her boss, her brows pinched in confusion. "What?"

Faith, who'd begun sifting through the mail, held up a cream-colored envelope, her confused expression mirroring Luna's. "It doesn't have a return address, but it's postmark is from Redding. Do you have family there?"

Luna almost laughed. Family. That was something other people had. She just shook her head and moved back to the counter, taking the thick envelope from her boss. "It's definitely not family. It's probably someone I went to school with or an old roommate."

Faith's eyebrows rose. "No family?"

Damn. Why had she said anything? Luna never talked about the fact that she didn't have any of her own people out there somewhere. Her past was just too depressing. Instead, she was always vague. It worked for her. Usually. "Not anymore. My mom passed away and it was just the two of us."

"Oh, Luna. I'm so sorry," Faith said, pressing her hand to her chest. "I didn't mean to pry."

"I know. It's all right." Luna gave her a reassuring smile before disappearing to her massage room. She held the envelope between two fingers and stared at it for a long moment. Nope. She wasn't ready to confront whatever past was coming back to haunt her. Tucking the envelope into her back pocket, she put the entire thing out of her mind. She had a client coming in twenty minutes. Time to get back to work.

When Luna was finally done with her last appointment of the day, she made her way down the hallway to Faith's office. After one knock on the closed door, she heard a faint, "Come in."

Luna had meant to just poke her head in, but just as she opened the door, Faith's private line rang. Faith reached over to pick it up, waved Luna in, and pointed to one of the overstuffed chairs in the sitting area.

"Faith Townsend," she said into the phone. Her normally sunny expression turned dark as she frowned. "No, Gabby. I already told you I'm not interested."

Luna perched on the edge of the seat, not sure if she should be there considering Faith's entire demeanor had just changed. Her shoulders were hunched, and her jaw clenched. Whoever was on the other end of the line had wound Faith tighter than she'd ever seen her.

"Well, that's for you to figure out," Faith continued. "It might be part of your program to try to make amends, but I'm under no obligation to make that easy for you." There was a pause, and Faith's eyes flashed with anger. "No, I'm not intentionally punishing you. Stop guilting me. I'm just not ready, all right?"

Luna stood, understanding she was eavesdropping on a personal conversation. "I'll wait outside," she whispered.

But Faith covered the receiver of the phone and shook her head. "No need. Give me a sec."

Since her boss had just insisted she stay, Luna sat back down and tried not to listen. She failed.

"I have to go," Faith said, her voice harsher than Luna had ever heard it. "No, I won't be coming... I don't know if Abby or Yvette would be interested." Faith pressed a hand to the back of her neck. "No, I doubt Noel will go either. I'm hanging up now." She started to lower the receiver, but Gabby must've yelled something into the phone, because Faith quickly pressed the phone back to her ear. "What did you just say?"

Luna stared at the wall, a chill crawling over her skin. After her unpleasant years in the foster system, Luna had developed a major aversion to the drama of family. And sitting in the office, listening to Faith deal with someone who was obviously family, started to make Luna's skin itch. She needed to get off the chair and just walk right out of the room. She'd make an excuse. It wasn't that hard. People did it all the time.

"You what?" Faith stood up, her eyes huge. "That's not possible. Hunter would know… I'm not listening to your lies. Goodbye, Gabby." She slammed the phone down, sank back into the chair, and rested her hands against her forehead.

Luna sat frozen, unsure of what to do. She wanted to give Faith a moment to process whatever she'd just heard, but at the same time, she wanted to give her privacy.

"Goddess. I'm so sorry, Luna." She looked up from her hands, her eyes glassy as if she were holding back tears. "That was…" Faith sucked in a shaky breath. "Well, it was unexpected." Straightening, she leveled her gaze at Luna. "What can I do for you?"

Luna let out a quiet chuckle. "I was just getting ready to call it a day and only stopped by to see if you need anything before I leave."

Faith's frustration and tension eased, causing her shoulders and jaw to relax slightly. "Dang, I lucked out when you applied, didn't I?" Her smile lit up her entire face as she pulled out a sheet of paper and pushed it to the edge of her desk. "All I need for you to do is sign this."

Luna leaned forward and grabbed what looked to be a contract. "What is this?"

"It's an employment agreement." Her smile widened. "You've been here long enough for us to know it's a good fit, right?"

"Sure." Luna nodded because she liked her job. Faith was easy to work for, and the customers were amazing.

"And you've just moved to town, so you're settled. Not leaving any time soon?" she asked.

"Yep, moved to town, not leaving," Luna confirmed.

"Excellent. Because I've decided the best way to keep great employees is by offering profit sharing incentives. Your base pay isn't changing. Well it is," she said with a nod of her head, "but that's because you're getting a raise. It's what we talked about when you were hired. But now you'll get bonuses based on the performance of the shop. How's that sound?"

Luna was certain she'd heard wrong. Bonuses? Profit sharing? Luna had only been there a short time. She knew she was a valued employee, and she was damned good at her job. She just hadn't expected... this. She cleared her throat. "That's very generous of you, Faith. Are you sure that's what you want to do? Not that I'm complaining, I just... I haven't been here long."

Faith moved from behind her desk and sat in the chair next to Luna's. She turned kind eyes on her employee. "Listen, I've already worked out that you don't like to talk about the past. That's fine. I have baggage I'm not exactly interested in revisiting either." She waved a hand at the phone. "You just got a peek at it with that call I wasn't expecting." Faith shook her head as if to dislodge the memory from her brain. "Anyway, I know you said you don't have family out there somewhere, and I have no intention of prying about that."

Luna opened her mouth but then realized she had no idea what to say. Thank you? Good? Drop it?

"I just want you to know that I think of everyone who works here as family. And when you're my family, the entire Townsend clan claims you," Faith said. "If you know anything about the Townsends, it's that we take care of family. Even when they don't want us to, so try to sidestep that one, okay?"

A surprise bubble of laughter rose from the back of Luna's throat. "I'll try my best."

"That's all anyone can do."

Faith stood and held her arms open. "Is it inappropriate to ask for a hug?"

"Yes," Luna said, still laughing. But she rose from her chair and gave Faith the hug she asked for. Luna sank into the other woman's embrace. It was warm and comfortable, and for the first time in forever, Luna didn't feel that edge of panic rising up and threatening to choke her. But her eyes did sting with tears from the unexpected gesture. "Thank you, Faith. You have no idea what this means to me."

"You're welcome." Faith pulled back, grinning at her. "Now go. I know you have a big date tonight. Don't want to keep that pretty musician waiting."

Luna's mouth dropped open. "You, too? Who told you?"

"Hanna. Why, was it a secret?"

"No. Everyone will see us together at dinner anyway. It just got around fast, that's all."

"Oh. Right." Faith patted her arm. "Don't blame Hanna. She only mentioned it after Shannon started talking about how she'd asked him out and he'd turned her down. Apparently, she was bugging Chad while he worked on his store and pried it out of him."

"He turned her down?" That knowledge made Luna's stomach flip over. "Shannon's gorgeous."

"So are you," Faith said. "Now go. I have a few things to finish up before I go find Hunter and make sure Ms. Betty hasn't hunted him down for another feel."

Luna was still laughing as she slipped out of the front door. It had been a great day. She just prayed she got through this *date* without making an idiot of herself.

CHAPTER 8

*W*hat did one wear for a date at the brewpub? Luna was guessing casual, but nice? Did that mean jeans and a clean top or a skirt and cute shoes? She rummaged through her meager wardrobe and let out a curse when she couldn't find the skirt she was looking for—the one that made her legs look amazing. Instead, she came up with a black number that was a little more witchy than she intended for a first date, but since it was less than twenty-four hours since she'd moved and most of her stuff was still waiting to be unpacked, she made do with what she had on hand.

After a quick shower, Luna pulled on black fishnet tights, the mostly tulle skirt, and a waist-cinching corset top that made her look two sizes smaller. She scanned the overall effect of the outfit and knew because she lived in Keating Hollow, she'd fit right in. But still, it seemed a little over the top for pub food. She glanced at herself again and decided she was going with it because, damn, she looked hot.

Chad wouldn't know what hit him. Chuckling to herself, she retreated to the bathroom to fix her hair and makeup.

Luna was just descending the stairs when she heard the knock on the door, feeling self-conscious for the first time since she'd put her ensemble together. She was nervous, and her hands had started to sweat.

"Relax, Hope," she whispered to herself. "It's just Chad." The truth was he'd seen her at her worst, and she wanted to rectify that. Just for pure self-satisfaction, no matter how trivial that sounded.

His knock sounded again. With her head held high, she went to open the door. And what she found was the most adorable man in pressed slacks and a short-sleeved button-down shirt, holding a bouquet of violet tulips.

"Hello, gorgeous," he said, his eyes twinkling with interest. "Nice dress."

She chuckled. "It's a skirt, but close enough. Come on in." Luna led him to her small kitchen where she rooted around for something to put the tulips in. "I don't think I have a vase."

"Got a milk container?" he asked.

"No." She opened her cabinet and pulled out a smoothie thermos. "I think this is the best I can find."

"It'll work." Chad filled the container with water and the tulips and put them on her counter. "Next time I'll be sure to get a vase, too."

Next time. If she'd been unsure before about the status of this outing, the flowers had provided clear clarification that this was indeed a date. And he was already anticipating a second one. Her heart did a little flip, causing her face to heat with a flush.

Chad glanced around at the mostly empty house. "What is your plan for furnishings?"

She took a breath and tried to act like her pulse hadn't started racing. After moving to Eureka and starting her new job, Luna's funds had gotten dangerously low. She needed to work on replenishing her savings before she went on any shopping sprees. "I was thinking I'd hit some yard sales or a couple of secondhand places when I get a chance. New furniture isn't really in the budget just yet."

"Sounds like a plan," he said with a nod. "You know, my stepmom has some things you might be interested in. She recently redecorated, and her garage is filled with furniture just waiting for the next yard sale. You should stop by and check if there's anything to your taste."

She smiled up at him. The man really didn't know how to stop taking care of people, did he? "I'll do that. Thanks."

"Ready for some food?" He held his arm out to her.

"Starving." She slipped her arm through his and glanced up at his handsome face as she let him lead her out of her newly rented place.

Keating Hollow Brewery was packed when Chad and Luna walked in ten minutes later. The bar was full, and there were groups of people waiting to be seated.

"Whoa," Luna said. "I wonder what's going on."

"Maybe Yvette is having another event at her bookstore," Chad offered.

Luna glanced around and spotted Abby Townsend hurrying toward them. She didn't normally work at the brewery, but since her father owned the place and her husband was the manager, she occasionally helped out when needed. She had an apron tied around her waist and was holding a stack of menus.

"Chad, Luna, hi!" she said with a bright smile. Her honey-blond hair was tied up in a long ponytail, and she had a cardamom scent as if she'd been baking... or more likely whipping up batches of her healing potions. She was a very successful earth witch who sold healing potions, lotions, and soaps. "Welcome to the circus. Need a table?"

"Looks like you're filled up," Chad said. "How long is the wait?"

"Is it just the two of you?"

"Yep." Chad reached out and put a hand on the small of Luna's back.

Tingles radiated up Luna's spine, and she suppressed the urge to shudder from his touch.

"I've got an open two-top in the back. The rest of these parties are three or more. Follow me."

They walked through the busy restaurant until they got to a small table in a quieter section of the pub. "How's this?" Abby asked.

"Perfect." Chad pulled a chair out for Luna and then took his seat across from her.

Abby's gaze had followed Chad's movements, and when he glanced back up to take one of the menus, she smiled knowingly at him. "Looks like it didn't take you long to ask out the prettiest girl in town."

Chad chuckled. "I wish that were true, but it turns out she asked me."

Abby's eyebrows rose. "Well, lucky you then."

"You've got that right." Chad smiled at Luna.

Luna felt her face flush again, and she mumbled, "It's just a thank-you dinner. Chad helped me move yesterday."

"That was sweet of you, Chad," Abby said with a kind smile. She handed Luna the other menu and took their drink orders.

When she was done rattling off the specials, Chad asked, "What's going on? Is there an event in town we don't know about?"

"You'd think so, right?" Abby said. "But nope. There was an

article that went viral online about the new brews Clay and Rhys have been working on. Ever since then, the place has been packed to the gills. People are coming from all over to check this place out. They've even filled up Noel's inn. It's crazy."

"Beer enthusiasts?" Luna asked.

Abby nodded. "It's pretty insane. I'm not sure what to make of it all."

"Just enjoy it I guess," Luna said with a smile.

Abby returned her smile and indicated she'd be back soon to get their dinner orders.

"So…" Luna started, nodding toward Chad's hand. He'd been flexing and stretching it ever since they walked into the restaurant. "Did you make an appointment for a massage?"

He glanced down at his hand and pressed his palm to the table as if to stop himself from doing the small exercises. It was almost as if he hadn't even known he'd been stretching his fingers out. "I did, but the spa is booked solid for the next three weeks."

"It is?" Luna asked in surprise. She knew the place was doing well. The days she worked, she was booked solid. But she had no idea the backlog was that long.

"You didn't know?" he asked.

She shook her head. "Lena runs the administration end."

"You're just the talent?" he teased, his eyes sparkling again.

Damn, he was gorgeous when he looked at her like that. He was so full of happy goodness that he was almost a drug. One she never wanted to give up. "Yeah, something like that," she said. "But you don't have to wait that long. Come in tomorrow morning. I'll squeeze you in before my first appointment of the day."

"You don't have to do that, Luna." But even as the words

sailed out of his mouth, he started massaging the joints between his knuckles.

She laughed. "You don't even realize you're doing that, do you?"

"Huh?" He glanced down at his hands. This time it was his turn to flush. His cheeks turned pink, and all she wanted to do in that moment was press her hands to his face and kiss him. Instead, she leaned back in her chair and tried to pretend she wasn't wildly attracted to this man who was ten years her senior and probably still saw her as the messed-up kid she'd been three years ago. He gave her a half smile. "I guess not. It's just a constant ache most of the time. My new normal."

"I'm not sure it has to be." Luna propped her elbows on the table and cradled her chin in her hands. "How long did you have relief after the short massage I gave you yesterday?"

He frowned, clearly mulling the question over. "I think I didn't notice the ache until this morning when I opened a jar for Barb. I'm staying in the apartment over the garage, and we usually have breakfast together."

Luna grinned. It was cute that he felt the need to explain his living situation. Of course, she'd already known where he was living. The small-town rumor mill didn't quiet for anyone. "That's good. The relief lasted for at least twelve hours, which is remarkable since it was agitated from the move. I don't want to get ahead of myself, but I think I can probably help you ease that chronic pain."

"I was already sold after yesterday's sample," he said with a chuckle. "Just tell me when and where, and I'll be there."

"We'll start with tomorrow morning and go from there."

Abby arrived with their drinks, took their burger orders, and promised their food would be right up. But Luna didn't care how long her food took, because for the first time in years, she felt herself relax and let herself enjoy the man across from her.

"Are you going to tell me how you hurt your hand?" Luna asked.

Chad's jaw tightened as he crumpled up a napkin in his fist, his knuckles going white from the effort.

"You don't have to talk about it," Luna insisted, trying desperately to back out of the question. "I'm sorry I asked. Forget it."

"No, it's okay. I'm just embarrassed, that's all," Chad admitted.

That got her attention. It wasn't the words; it was the way he said them. He wasn't talking about some silly accident. This was about shame. She lowered her voice and stared him right in the eye as she surprised herself by saying, "It's all right, Chad. Whatever it is, it can't be worse than what I've done."

Chad's expression turned to one of surprise but quickly softened. He reached across the table and slipped his good hand over one of hers. "I'm not so sure about that. But can we talk about this after dinner? Somewhere quieter, maybe?"

She glanced around the crowded pub and nodded. She wouldn't want to spill her secrets there either.

When their burgers arrived, Luna took a bite and let out a small moan of pleasure. The Townsends sourced their ingredients from small local farms and served grass fed beef. Fresh and flavorful were understatements.

"Agreed," Chad said with a nod.

Luna put her burger down and took a long sip of her tea. Nibbling on a fry, she said, "Let's talk about your music shop. What are your plans?"

As they continued to dig into their dinner, Chad launched into a detailed marketing plan that involved selling instruments, teaching piano, and bringing in guest artists for meet-and-greets and even organizing some concerts down by the river.

"Sounds ambitious and wonderful for Keating Hollow," Luna said, admiring his willingness to invest in the community. It was just like him, though. Even though he'd traveled a lot for concerts when he'd lived in Berkeley, he still spent a lot of time down at the local community center, volunteering by giving piano lessons to the kids who came in after school.

He shrugged. "It's a way to stay involved in music."

"Your first love." She smiled at him.

Chad hesitated for a moment as if he were contemplating exactly who or what his first love was, but then he let out a chuckle and nodded. "You're probably right about that. Piano saved me when I was a teenager. I don't know where I would've ended up without it."

"Really?" Luna sat up. "Do you think you would've turned into a hoodlum like I did?"

Chad raised one eyebrow at that.

"Well, it's true, isn't it?" she said, almost defiantly. Considering her past wasn't anything she ever wanted to talk about, she'd surprised herself by bringing it up. But for some reason, she felt like she needed him to acknowledge what she'd done and not keep ignoring the elephant in the room.

"No. It isn't," he insisted. "You were never a criminal, Luna. You were a kid stuck in a bad situation and shit got real."

Abby appeared with the check, and without even looking at the bill, Chad handed her a credit card.

"You can't just pretend none of that happened," Luna challenged. "Just because you saw me as a good kid, that doesn't mean I actually was." She leaned across the table and lowered her voice. "There's a reason I spent time in juvy, Chad."

"There certainly is, but it's not because of—"

Abby reappeared. "Thanks, you two. Enjoy the rest of your evening."

"Thanks, Abby," Chad said, smiling up at her. "Everything was great as usual."

She beamed and waved as she took off to deal with other tables.

Chad added the tip, signed the bill, and stood, holding his hand out to Luna. "Come on. Let's walk. There are some things we need to clear up."

Luna stared at his hand, torn between wanting to clasp it and wanting to bolt. She'd come to terms with who and what she was. She didn't need him to tell her differently.

"Please," he said softly. "I have things you need to know."

She'd been about to get up and walk out, but the earnest expression on his face touched something deep inside of her. Chad was an honorable man. She was sure of it, and she suddenly desperately wanted to know what it was he had to say. "All right."

She placed her hand in his and let him lead her out onto the cobbled sidewalks of Keating Hollow. The sun had just set, and the town was bathed in twilight. Chad was silent as they walked toward the river. Whatever it was he needed to say, he was obviously gathering his thoughts.

Luna let him take as much time as he needed. As much as she wanted to hear what he had to say, she was in no hurry to take a trip down memory lane.

But it was too late. Walking next to him, smelling his familiar woodsy scent, everything she'd tried to bury came roaring back.

CHAPTER 9

BERKELEY, THREE YEARS EARLIER

*D*espite it being June, there was a chill in the air, and Hope shivered. She'd forgotten her sweater back at Starbucks where she'd just ended a seven-hour shift. But she ignored the cold. Chad had called her a half hour earlier and asked her to stop by his house on her way home.

Chad never called her. Not at home and not at her job. But he was always there for her when she needed him. Always. Now she wondered what it was he needed from her. If she was honest with herself, she hoped it meant he was interested in more than just the platonic friendship they had going on. Maybe he needed a date to one of his charity functions. It didn't matter to her that she was still seventeen. She'd just graduated high school. Wasn't that good enough?

Probably not, she told herself. Chad was far too decent and honorable to consider dating a teenager. Especially one who was a product of the foster care system. Maybe once she moved into his spare bedroom when she turned eighteen, he'd start to see her as an adult, instead of a ward of the state. Hope's living situation was perilous at best. Her foster mother didn't care about anyone. Not even her own biological kid, who'd finally stopped coming to visit.

Casey, her son, used to come by and do chores for her, stock her refrigerator, make sure she was doing all right, but when Pam hooked up with Leo, the mother-son relationship had gone straight into the toilet. Leo was a controlling son of a bitch who verbally abused the foster kids and physically abused Pam. But no matter what anyone said, she wouldn't do anything about it. She said Leo kept her safe and her light bill paid. After Casey and Leo got into a physical altercation over the bruise on his mother's eye, Pam took Leo's side, and Casey had split. No one could blame him.

Hope would've split too if she'd had anywhere to go. That night, as she did most nights, she'd ended up on Chad's front steps, venting about her living situation. She'd have moved out that minute if she could have found someone who'd let her rent a room. But no one wanted to deal with child services or someone who was underage. And all of her friends from school were headed off to college. Hope had gotten into a state school, but her grades weren't good enough for academic scholarships, and somehow her application for need-based help had gotten lost. Hope suspected sabotage by Leo, but she didn't have any proof.

"I don't know how or where yet, but you better believe that as soon as I turn eighteen and am no longer a ward of the state, I'm moving out," Hope insisted. "I can't stay in that house. Leo is too much of a loose cannon."

Chad leaned back in the porch swing, contemplating what she'd said. "Do you have any friends who can rent you a room?"

She shook her head. "They're all headed off to college. It's going to be tricky, because I'll only need a place until January. Maybe I can find a cheap monthly Airbnb for those few months. By then I'll have my financial situation worked out with the college, and I'll be out of here, too."

He glanced at his small house and hesitantly asked, "Would it be weird if I offered you my spare bedroom?"

She froze, staring at him as if he'd just spoken a foreign language. She swallowed the sudden lump in her throat. "Did you just offer for me to stay here?"

"It is weird." He grimaced. "I was just thinking that I have extra space I'm not using, and I hate the idea of you using the money you're saving for college on an Airbnb. But I don't want you to be uncomfortable. Just forget it."

"Forget it? Hell no!" She jumped up and threw herself into the swing and hugged him with everything she had. Her chest was heavy with emotion as tears stung the backs of her eyes. "You're the best friend I've ever had. Do you know that?"

He let out a soft chuckle. But then he turned serious. "I am honored to call you a friend, Hope."

She'd clung to him for what seemed like forever. Then she'd wiped her eyes and steeled her resolve to get through the next three months until she was free of the system.

Two weeks later, when Chad called her at work to tell her he needed to talk to her, she went straight to his house and was surprised not to find him waiting for her on his porch the way he usually did. She knocked, and when he answered, he looked haggard, like he hadn't slept the night before.

"Hey. Come in. There's pasta on the stove if you're hungry." He led the way to the small kitchen and took a seat at the table, holding his head with one hand.

"What's wrong?" she asked, sitting across from him.

"I have news."

She waited, her pulse kicking up. Was he sick? Did he have a family emergency? "Are you all right? Can I do anything to help?"

His regretful gaze met hers. "I'm so sorry, Hope. I found out yesterday that my contract isn't going to be renewed with the symphony here."

"You're losing your job? They can't just fire you. You're like some sort of prodigy," she argued, unable to believe anyone would let him go. He played the piano like an angel.

"They didn't fire me. The company is disbanding. No one got a new contract," he said, sounding miserable.

"Oh. That really sucks," she said, wanting to reach out and grab his hand, but one was still holding his head up and the other must've been resting on his knee under the table. Instead she gave him an encouraging smile and said, "I'm sure you'll land on your feet. You're you for goodness sake."

"I already have a new contract," he said, sounding miserable.

She sat back, frowning at him. "Okay. Then why do you look like someone kicked your puppy?"

"It's in Chicago. I have to leave tonight on the red eye."

His words hung between them as the air got sucked right out of the room. This couldn't be happening. Her birthday was just shy of three months away, and she'd gotten used to the idea of moving in with Chad. Everything was set in her mind. She'd even started looking for second-hand furniture for his empty spare room. "And this house?" she finally forced out. "When does the lease run out?"

"It's a month to month." He grimaced. "I'm so sorry, Hope. I'd keep the lease if I could, but I can't afford this and a place in

Chicago. I'm sorry. I know this really messes things up for you."

And there was no way she could afford to foot the rent for the next six months. Not if she wanted funds for her college apartment. That meant three to six more months of her foster mother's house if she couldn't find anywhere else. She closed her eyes and prayed she wouldn't cry. *It won't be that bad,* she told herself. Pam would make her pay a little rent, but she could manage with some extra shifts at her job. "It's all right. I've survived this long. It was kind of you to offer your house, Chad. I appreciate everything you've done for me more than you know."

They hugged and wished each other well, and then Hope ran out of there before she completely broke down. Once she was back in Pam's house, she headed straight for the tiny room she shared with another foster kid and climbed into the top bunk, ready to cry her eyes out. Besides losing her place to stay, her best friend was leaving, and she wasn't sure she'd ever see him again.

"Hope!" Pam cried from somewhere in the house.

Rolling over, Hope ignored her. Maybe Pam would assume she wasn't home.

"Hope! Get your ass out here. I have an errand for you to run."

"No effing way," she muttered and clutched her pillow.

The door slammed open and Pam's cheap high heels clacked against the hardwood floors right before she reached up and grabbed Hope's ankle and yanked. "Get your lazy butt up. I have something for you to do. Now."

"Go away, Pam," Hope said without any heat in her voice. Couldn't the woman see that Hope was heartbroken? Actually, she probably didn't. Pam only saw what she wanted to see, and in that moment, Hope was a means to an end.

"Get your ass out of that bed or you'll never see this box of cash again," Pam threatened.

Hope flipped over and sat straight up, her eyes widening in fear as she spotted her cash box, the one she kept under the floorboard in her closet. "Where did you get that?" Hope demanded as she flew off the bed and lunged for it. "That's mine. I worked hard for that money."

Pam just laughed and let her take the box.

Hope knew the moment she grabbed the box that it was empty. The money didn't slide around, and it felt awful light. In addition to paper money, Hope had collected quarters. "What did you do with my school money?"

Pam stood there smirking in too tight jeans, a white tank top, and a cigarette dangling out of her mouth. "Relax, princess. It's safe. I just needed insurance that you'd run my little errand. All you need to do is deliver my latest potions to Ricky, and then you can have your precious college money back. Though I am going to take some out for rent."

"Rent! I'm still a ward of the state," Hope insisted.

"You aren't in three months when you turn eighteen," Pam said with a sickly sweet smile. "The checks will stop, and that means no more money is coming from the state while you spend the fall here. You'll officially be a freeloader. Unless you want to pack up on your birthday and head out, you'll start contributing when I tell you to."

Hatred was an emotion that Hope actively tried to avoid. It was tough when almost everyone in your life was a jackass, but she'd been conscious of trying to let her frustrations go. But that night, staring at Pam, hatred filled every pore of Hope's being, and she wanted to claw the woman's eyes out. How dare she touch Hope's money and blackmail her into transporting her potions. Illegal potions that were used by the magical community to get high.

"Whatever," Hope barked. "Give me the damn potions so I can get this over with. And give me my money back now."

"You'll get it when you get back," Pam said.

Hope glared at her, knowing full well that the woman could be bluffing. There was a reason Hope hid the money in the first place. When she'd found out she couldn't get a bank account without a guardian's signature, she'd nixed that idea. If Pam was on the account, her money would be gone minutes after she deposited it, so she'd decided to keep her cash hidden. Unfortunately, she hadn't hidden it well enough. Now her only chance of getting it back was to transport Pam's illegal potions. *Damn.* "It had all better be there or—"

"Or what? You'll leave? You'll turn me in? You'll call your social worker? Honey, you age out in a few weeks. No one is worried about you. And if you think I won't bring you down with me if you call the cops, think again. Just do your job and let me worry about that stack of cash you've built up."

Hope wanted to strangle her but managed to refrain. She needed to play nice until she had her apartment money back in her possession. "Where are the potions?"

"Follow me," Pam said.

An hour later, Hope arrived at Ricky's place of business in the warehouse district, potions in hand. The sleazy bastard patted her down before he'd let her in the garage he used as his home base and then proceeded to talk about what great assets she had. Hope ignored him, waiting out his disgusting diatribe until he got bored and finally paid her for the delivery. She was rushing out when the cops showed up. She went to jail that night, along with Ricky and three of his crew members. She stayed locked up until her eighteenth birthday.

When she was released, a courier met her outside the station with a box. It contained the money Pam had taken from her and paperwork for a short-term rental for a month. That was it. No note. No explanation. She assumed Pam had an attack of conscience for landing her in jail but hadn't wanted her back at her house, and this was her way of absolving herself.

Hope had never forgiven her, but the money and the short-term rental had helped her when she needed it most, and she was grateful for the gesture.

CHAPTER 10

*C*had and Luna sat on a bench facing the river. He stared at Luna's lovely profile and ached to brush his fingers over her cheek. The teenager he'd gotten to know during his time in Berkeley had turned into a strong, talented woman. One he admired more than anyone else he knew. Her quiet strength captivated him, and he knew if he wanted a chance at any sort of relationship, friendly or romantic, she needed the truth.

"Remember when I told you it was my fault you ended up in juvy?" he asked.

"Yeah. And I told you it wasn't," she said quietly. "How could it be? You were on your way to Chicago."

He closed his eyes and spoke the truth he'd been carrying around for three years. "I'm the one who tipped off the police about the potions and told them I knew about an exchange happening that night at Ricky's place."

Chad felt Luna stiffen beside him, and when he opened his eyes, he saw her burning with betrayal. She jumped to her feet and glared down at him. "You... why? Why would you do that,

Chad? Hadn't you already hurt me enough? Do you have any idea what that night did to me? I lost everything that was important to me that night. I didn't have much, but I had a future and a plan, and I thought I had at least one friend out there who cared about me even if he was getting on a plane."

"I didn't know Pam was going to make you deliver her potions," he said, the words coming out in a rush. "I didn't think you ever did that."

"I didn't!" she yelled. "But isn't it crazy that the one night she basically forced me to do it, I'm the one who ended up going to jail?"

He'd had that same thought more times than he could count. "Listen, I'd like to explain if—"

"What's to explain?" she asked, her voice full of heat. "You were leaving town and decided to butt in where you didn't belong, and I paid the price. Is there anything else I need to know?"

"Yes, there is," he said, turning to face her and staring her in the eye. "I did it to try to help you. Do you have any idea how upset I was that you were going to be there in that house with no one to watch over you, no one to stand in Leo's way if he decided he wanted to do more than just leer at you?"

"I was there for years, Chad. He never touched me," she said. But she shuddered because she'd always thought he was capable.

"You know why he didn't, Hope?" He heard her real name on his lips and winced. "Sorry, Luna."

She waved an impatient hand. "It hardly matters now. I chose a new name to escape my past, but it appears that's going to be impossible. Not with you here to remind me of it every day." Luna gritted her teeth as she addressed his question. "I always thought he left me alone because I'd made it clear I'd rip his balls off with my bare hands if he tried anything."

Chad smiled at her, and he couldn't stop himself from wrapping his hands around her bare arms as he said, "That was probably a factor. But I think he also stayed away from you because I never wasted a chance to let him know that I was watching him. I might have implied that my father had business associates he wouldn't want to meet in a dark alley."

Luna's eyes widened. "You did? How is it he never beat the shit out of you?"

"He knew my father," Chad said, his expression darkening in the moonlight.

"Do I want to know who he was?" Luna asked.

Chad shook his head and flexed his aching hand. "When I knew I was leaving, I was worried that jackass would try something. I overheard him and Pam talking about a potions exchange. Leo was supposed to make the drop off. I swear to the gods, Luna, if I'd had any clue Pam was going to force you to do it, I'd have never done anything to get you in trouble. All I wanted to do was get Leo away from you."

To his surprise, Luna sank back down onto the bench he was sitting on and let out a deep sigh. "You were just looking out for me, like you always did."

"Yes. I should've told you." He'd been such a bundle of nerves that day. After being blindsided by the news that his orchestra was dismantling and that there a contract waiting for him in another city as long as he got there by the next day, his thoughts had been whirling. He could handle moving. But what about Hope? He'd been twisted up inside about leaving her behind in her horrible living situation. Then he'd acted rashly and gotten her in trouble.

77

"Yeah, that would've helped," she agreed. "But then, you likely didn't believe I'd ever be involved in any of that."

"No, I didn't. That's not you."

"It's not." She reached over and squeezed his good hand. "Thank you for believing in me."

"I always did." He squeezed her hand and held on, not wanting to let her go.

"She stole my school money," Luna said. "That's why I did it. She said she'd give it back once I made the exchange."

He'd learned that the night she'd been arrested, but it didn't seem like the time to bring it up. He wanted to hear what else she had to say. "Did you believe her?"

Luna let out a bark of humorless laughter. "No. But I had to try. I was desperate. Those people did everything in their power to keep me from going to college. In the end, they got their wish."

"But you managed massage therapy school," he said. "That's something to be proud of."

"Sure." She leaned back against the bench and then slid toward him until her head was resting on his shoulder. "But they stole my opportunity to be a normal kid at college where no one knew I was the poor foster kid. It's something I won't ever get back."

"Is that why you don't want anyone in Keating Hollow to know about your past? So you can just be you on your own terms, without any labels or preconceived notions?" He was really curious. Because in his eyes, she had absolutely nothing to be ashamed of. Her past only made him admire her more for what she'd become.

"Yeah. But I also don't want Faith to know I was incarcerated. The records are sealed since I was a juvenile, so it's not something that shows up in a background check. And the last thing I want is for her to think I used to be some sort of criminal when I was really just a kid trying to survive a crappy foster home."

Chad wrapped an arm around her shoulders and pulled her closer for a sideways hug. "I understand." He held up his injured hand. "I wouldn't want anyone to know about the circumstances of how I managed this mess either."

She took his hand between both of hers and started to massage.

He let out a small moan of approval. "That feels really good."

"I know." She grinned up at him. "Are you going to tell me what happened or…"

He pulled away slightly. "Yeah. That's—" His phone started to ring. "Hold on." After fishing the device out of his pocket, he frowned. He didn't recognize the number. "Hello?"

"Um, Chad?" a voice he didn't recognize said over the connection.

"Yes. Who's this?"

"It's Levi," the kid said as his voice cracked. There was a sniffle before he added, "I need help."

Chad grabbed Luna's hand and pulled her to her feet as he stood. He was already tugging her back toward town when he asked Levi, "Where are you?"

"Parking lot of Pies, Pies, and More Pies." The kid's teeth were chattering, but Chad knew that unless it was twenty degrees cooler in Eureka, it wasn't nearly cold enough for someone to be that chilled.

"Are you safe?" Chad asked.

"I don't… I don't know," he said.

"Do I need to call 911?"

"911?" Luna asked in a loud whisper. "What's happening?"

79

Chad shook his head. He had no idea. All he knew was that Levi sounded like he was scared and possibly in shock. "I'm on my way, Levi. Hang tight. If you need medical attention, just say the word. I'll call someone to help."

"No doctors," the kid insisted and then hung up.

Chad cursed and sped up. "That was Levi. He's in some sort of trouble. I need to go get him."

"I'll come with you," Luna insisted.

"No, you don't have to do that. It's a couple hours roundtrip, and that's only if he doesn't need to see the inside of a hospital. I'll drop you at your place so you can get some rest. You have a busy day tomorrow, remember?"

"Chad, come on. I'm not going to get to sleep until I know he's okay anyway."

He nodded. "All right."

CHAPTER 11

*L*una's stomach was in knots. It had been forty minutes since Chad answered Levi's call, and the worst sort of scenarios kept playing in her mind. What if he was caught up with selling drugs, or worse, prostitution? If he truly was a homeless teen, both were a more-than-likely possibility. She just wanted to wrap her arms around him, take him home, and reassure him everything would be all right.

Her wishes were naïve. She knew that better than anyone. Whatever trouble he was in would take a lot more than just a warm bed and a hot meal to fix. But she was willing to do whatever she could for him if he'd let her. Calling Chad had been the first step.

Chad swung the truck into the packed parking lot of Pies, Pies, and More Pies and swore. "Why is this place so busy at ten at night?"

"It's because of the movie theater," Luna said. "The patrons have started coming here for pie before heading home for the evening."

Chad's grip tightened on the wheel as he turned down the far row, looking for a place to park. "I just hope he's still here."

"Let me out," Luna insisted. "I'll start scanning the area and will text when I spot him."

"I don't think that's a good idea. What if whatever trouble he's in followed him here?" Chad said.

Luna rolled her eyes. "There are people everywhere, Chad. I'll scream and make the biggest nuisance of myself you've ever seen. Please. I'm worried he's hurt."

Still unable to find a spot, Chad jerked the truck to a stop. "Be careful and text me if you see anything remotely unusual."

"I will." She jumped out of the truck and started trotting toward the building. Putting herself in Levi's situation, she knew if she'd called someone because she was scared and needed help, she'd probably be tucked away somewhere out of view. Somewhere like behind the building, near the dumpsters. But when she rounded the corner, the only thing she spotted was a dumpster with garbage bags overflowing from the top.

After carefully checking the area, she trotted to the other side of the building and frowned. Something felt off, but she couldn't zero in on what it could be. The side of the building faced an undeveloped field that had a chain link fence around it. Unless he was lying in a patch of overgrown grass, he wasn't on that side of the building either.

She was just getting ready to round the corner back toward the main parking lot when the hair stood up on the back of her neck. She froze and then slowly scanned the seemingly deserted area.

Levi was there somewhere. She knew it deep in her gut.

A rustling sound came from somewhere off to her right. She squinted into the darkness and spotted a door in the side of the building that had been cracked open. Coming from the other direction, she hadn't even realized the door had existed.

There.

She broke out into a run, her blood pounding in her ears. The air seemed to change around her. It was sparking with magic and making her skin crawl with unease. What was happening? Her stomach rolled, and she half expected to lose her burger. But she pressed a hand to her stomach, her own magic spreading over her skin and calming her insides.

"No! Don't," a boy said with a whimper. The voice was faint, but it was definitely Levi's.

Luna's heart raced. Someone was hurting him. She whipped out her phone and sent Chad a quick text letting him know her location and that Levi was in trouble. Then she flipped her ringer to silent and barreled straight through the cracked door.

The magic thickened around her, making her head dizzy.

"Luna," Levi said with a gasp. "Help me."

"Shut up, you ungrateful bastard. Do you have any idea where your homo ass would be if I hadn't taken you in?" a deeper voice growled.

Luna blinked. She saw nothing but an empty hallway. But her vision was blurry, and she couldn't seem to focus. Was this some sort of illusion spell? Levi and some other guy were clearly nearby, but they were invisible to her.

Taking a step forward, she pushed her arms out in front of her, trying to feel what she couldn't see.

"Luna," Levi gasped out. "No. Get out of here. It's not safe."

The sound of flesh smacking flesh rang in Luna's ears. Levi let out a cry and then moaned. Unmitigated rage seized Luna, and instead of heeding his warning, she ran straight down the hallway, hand out until a rock-hard hand wrapped around her wrist and jerked her to a stop. It had been dumb to go in blind. She knew that. But leaving Levi on his own to be tortured by his abuser was unthinkable.

"Hello, princess," the deep voice said in her ear.

Years of defending herself while being bounced around from one foster home to another kicked in, and Luna rounded on her captor, using her free hand to smash her palm into his nose. The minute the connection was made, the blurry illusion spell vanished, and the messy storage room came into view. There was no time to look around, though, because the man who was holding her wrist twisted her arm behind her back, nearly sending her to her knees. Instead, she steeled herself and stomped down hard on his instep, and when he loosened his hold, she threw her elbow back, slamming it right into his eye.

"You god dammed bi—augh!"

Luna landed a roundhouse kick right in his gut. When he doubled over, she brought both hands down, pummeling him on the back of his head. The man fell to the floor, his limbs still as he moaned.

"What the... Holy hell, Luna," Chad said from behind her, his voice awed.

"It turns out foster homes are good for at least one thing," she said as she turned and scanned the dimly lit room for Levi. He was pressed against a storage shelf, blood coating the side of his face and his eyes wild with fear as he tried frantically to get a hose untied from around his arm. Her eyes widened as she spotted a discarded needle lying on the ground.

She ran to his side. "Dammit, Levi. What did you take?"

"Nothing," he cried, flinging the rubber hose away from him as he scrambled away from the drug paraphernalia. "He was trying to drug me against my will. Get me out of here!"

Without a word, Chad strode forward and easily lifted the young man into his arms, cradling him against his chest. "It's all right, Levi. I've got you."

Levi was stiff with fear radiating from practically every pore.

"It's all right, Levi," Luna said softly, placing a calming hand on his arm. "Chad is someone you can trust. I promise."

Levi squeezed his fearful brown eyes shut, and after a moment, he let himself relax against Chad's broad chest.

"We need to get out of here," Chad said. "Before the ass clown wakes up."

Luna stalked over to the discarded needle and used the heal of her boot to crush it before following Chad out of the building.

The parking lot was still overflowing with cars, and Chad had doubled parked next to the dumpster area. By the time they were settled back into the vehicle, there was a line of cars jockeying for his non-existent spot.

"That's a mess," Luna said. She was sitting in the middle between Chad and Levi. But her full attention was on the boy. Silent tears were streaming down his face. There were fresh bruises on his neck and faded ones on his upper arms that looked like fingers where someone had grabbed him. She gently took his hand in hers and ran her fingers lightly over his arm, sending a bit of her healing magic over his skin. "Just try to relax. We're going to get you to a hospital to get your head checked out."

"No hospitals!" he cried, jerking his hand out of hers and grappling for the door handle.

"Whoa, Levi." She reached across and took both of his hands in hers and twisted so she could make eye contact. "You're going to be okay. I promise. We won't make you do anything you don't want to do. We just want to make sure your injuries aren't serious."

"I'll be fine," he said, even as he pulled one of his hands away and pressed his palm to his head. He winced and then grimaced as his hand came away sticky with blood.

"You're not fine. I think you hit your head. You might need stitches, and there's a possibility of a concussion. You need medical attention. What is it about hospitals that freak you out?"

"Hospitals aren't safe," he whispered.

Luna glanced at Chad. Their eyes met, both of them worried.

"How about a healer?" Luna tried. "There's a couple in Keating Hollow. A husband and wife team. They are very well respected."

"I don't know," he said, squeezing his eyes shut again. "I don't want to go back into the system."

Luna's heart nearly broke in half. She knew what it was like to trust no one in her life. "Head to Keating Hollow," she said to Chad. "We'll figure out what to do after he sees the Whipples."

"Already pointed in that direction." Chad dropped his hand onto her thigh in a reassuring gesture.

Luna pressed her hand to the back of his just for the connection. Then she sent a text to the Whipples letting them know they were bringing someone in. A return text said they'd meet them at the clinic.

Letting out a sigh of relief, Luna turned her attention back to Levi. "Don't worry about anything, Levi. You're safe with us. No one is sending you anywhere, understand?"

"Okay," he mumbled.

She wasn't sure he'd actually heard what she'd said, but he was no longer freaking out, and that was good enough for her.

"Luna?" Levi asked, his eyes fluttering open for just a moment.

"Yes?"

"Can you do that thing you did with your fingers again? It… felt nice."

"Of course." She reached over and trailed her fingers over his arm, letting a faint trace of her magic dance over his skin.

A tiny shudder shook him, but then his shoulders relaxed and the tension around his mouth eased.

"That's it," she soothed. "Feeling a little better?"

He nodded.

"Good. I'm glad."

Everyone was quiet while Chad navigated the highway that led back to Keating Hollow. Luna stared out the window at the moonlight reflecting on the roadside river and continued to hold Levi's hand, wishing she could take all of his pain away. But he needed a professional to take a look at his head. After he got a clean bill of health, she'd see if she could help with what must've been a massive headache.

"I don't do drugs or potions," Levi said into the silence.

Taken a little aback by his sudden announcement, she just patted his hand. "That's a good choice."

"My uncle wanted me to work for him. When I refused, we got into a physical fight and I bolted. He doesn't usually follow me, but this time he did, and he found me leaning against the Pies, Pies, and More Pies building while I waited for Chad."

"What happened when he found you?" Luna asked just to keep him talking. She could guess at the evening's events.

"He punched me and dragged me around the building and

into that storage room. He's been letting me crash on his couch, but he told me if I wanted to stay, I needed to earn my keep by helping him with his business. When I said no, he got angry and tried to force me into the life. That's his way, you know. Get kids hooked on that crap and then enlist them to move his product."

"That's horrible," Luna said, her chest heavy with both sadness and disgust. "Is he your real uncle?"

"Yes. My dad's brother. They don't speak." Levi leaned his head against Luna's shoulder and crossed his arms over his chest.

She wanted to ask where his father was and why Levi wasn't with him, but she kept her questions to herself. Now wasn't the time. If he was forced to live with an abusive uncle, he hadn't ended up there by choice. So instead of questioning him further, she wrapped an arm around his shoulders and held on as if she were keeping him from breaking apart.

As promised, Gerry Whipple was already at the clinic when they arrived. Gerry was a tall woman with short gray hair and kind eyes. She met them at the door and ushered the three of them back to her office, indicating that Luna and Chad should wait there while she checked on Levi's injuries.

"No!" Levi cried, panic in his eyes. "I'm saying with Luna."

Gerry turned to glance at Luna with her eyebrows raised.

She mouthed back, *Trust issues.*

"How about we take Luna with us?" Gerry asked.

He stared at the ground. "All right."

"Chad, will you be okay here while we get Levi patched up?" Gerry asked.

"Yep." He sat back in a chair and closed his eyes.

Luna pressed a hand to his shoulder and then got up to follow Levi and Gerry.

"Okay, Levi," Gerry said as she opened the door to the exam

room. "We'll be in there. I need you to get undressed and put one of these on." She handed him a paper gown. "Luna and I will wait outside to give you some privacy."

He swallowed thickly and averted his gaze, but he nodded.

"Take as much time as you need," Gerry said kindly. Then she ushered Luna out of the room and the pair of them sat in a couple of plastic chairs at the end of the hallway. "What can you tell me about what happened to him?"

"Not a lot. He was beaten by his uncle and almost shot up with some sort of drug or potion. He says we got there in time before he was drugged, though."

"Are you certain he isn't a user?" she asked.

Luna shook her head. "He says he doesn't do drugs, but honestly, Chad and I barely know him. We met him the other day when Chad was helping me move. It's obvious he's not in a great situation, so Chad gave him a business card and told him to call if he needed anything. We got the call tonight and went and picked him up in Eureka."

Gerry tapped her pen on her clipboard. "Do we need to call Child Protective Services?"

Luna grimaced. "I don't want to get you into any sort of trouble legally, but if there is any way we can hold off on that, I'd appreciate it. The kid is terrified. And honestly, Gerry, he has reason to be. I don't know his particular circumstances, but often the system isn't kind to teenagers. I'd like to just give him a safe place to sleep for the night and then try to decide what to do."

"You sound like you've had experience with this before," she said, eyeing Luna quizzically.

"You could say that." Luna didn't want to talk about her past, though she would if she had to in order to convince Gerry not to call anyone. "Listen. Just put down on his paperwork that I'm his aunt or something. If there's a problem later, I'll take the heat for it."

Gerry tapped the pen some more, thinking. "All right. But if I hear of any criminal activity from his legal guardian, I'll be obligated to call someone. Understood?"

Luna's gut churned. She didn't know if Levi's uncle was his legal guardian or not. But the chances of Levi telling Gerry anything seemed slim at best. He'd been right to be terrified to go to the hospital. They'd take one look at his injuries and call in everyone. Gerry, as a healer, didn't have as many regulations, but she still had standards and ethics. Luna admired that about her even if she did wish the woman would turn a blind eye just this once.

"I understand," Luna said. "I just ask that you consider the fact that even though everyone always has the best of intentions sometimes that call actually puts a kid back in a dangerous situation. All Chad and I want for him is a warm safe place to sleep and a chance to move on from his current hell."

Gerry gave her a sad smile. "I do understand, dear. Now come on. Let's see if we can't patch up that young man."

CHAPTER 12

*M*emories of Chad's childhood came roaring back with a vengeance. The yelling. The bruises. The terror he'd felt when his stepfather was drinking. The cast he'd worn for six weeks the summer before he turned thirteen. And the shame that he'd let it happen.

Chad had loved his mother with everything he had. She was his biggest supporter, his best friend, and the person he admired most. His stepfather, on the other hand... He'd been terrified of the man. He was a master manipulator who had everyone fooled. Everyone except Chad.

Hugh Russell had been the kind of guy who could charm the pants off anyone. He was clean-cut, friendly, and funny when he wanted to be. But when he had too many drinks, he was mean, jealous, and downright cruel. Since Chad's mother Frannie didn't approve of Hugh's drinking, he never indulged when she was home, which meant he waited until she worked her rotating night shifts to get really wasted. And mean.

The man hated Chad's relationship with his mother. Jealous bastard. Frannie was always happiest on the days when she and

Chad got to spend some one-on-one time together. They watched trashy television together, texted multiple times a day, and laughed a lot. All of Hugh's laughing was usually at his mother's expense, and Chad made no secret of how much he disapproved of that. In return, Hugh had gifted him with a black eye and told him if he breathed a word of where the bruise came from, he'd make sure Frannie had a collection of her own as well.

At thirteen years old, Chad had believed him.

Every time Hugh hurt Chad, he threatened to do the same to Frannie, and it had been an effective way to keep Chad under control. In fact, nothing changed until Chad was accepted into an elite music program in the city and left home to live on campus. He'd tried to tell his mother once, but Hugh had arrived unexpectedly and put the fear of the gods in him. He'd never spoken of it again.

Chad could still feel the incredible sense of helplessness he'd had as a kid, unable to do anything about his circumstances. He imagined Levi felt similar. All Chad wanted to do was protect the kid in a way that no one had been able to protect him.

The door creaked open, and Luna walked in. Her eyes were tired, and her shoulders were slightly hunched with fatigue.

"Hey," Chad said, patting the chair next to him. "Take a seat."

Luna did as he said and let out a heavy sigh. "Gerry's stitching up his head now. She said he'd need ten to twelve stitches, and we need to watch for concussion symptoms."

"Ouch." Chad rubbed his own head in sympathy.

Her voice cracked as she added, "There's also a sprained wrist, a bruised rib, and a cut on his cheek. Gerry says those should heal fairly quickly, but he's going to be in some pain for a few days."

"Did she prescribe a potion for the pain?" Chad asked, grateful it appeared Levi would be okay. His injuries were bad enough, but considering what they'd walked in on, things could've been way worse.

"Not yet. She said she wanted to run a tox screen just to make absolutely sure there isn't anything in his system." She rubbed at her temples. "I know she has to before offering any pain relievers, but I hate that he'll see it as a lack of trust."

Chad placed his palm over her open one and laced his fingers between hers. "I'm sure he understands on an intellectual level."

"It's his heart I'm worried about," she said, glancing over at him, weariness in her expression.

Gods. He knew exactly what she meant, and in that moment, all he wanted to do was wrap her in his arms and make both of their pasts fade into the background. Create a safe place within each other that had room for one scared teen. But he was getting ahead of himself, and the only one he should be worried about was Levi. "Me, too, Luna. But we can work on protecting him together, right?"

"I really hope so," she said, staring at their connected hands.

He squeezed her fingers. She glanced up, a hint of smile curving her lips, and she squeezed back. His heart fluttered, and he ached to lean in and kiss her. But now was not the time or the place.

The door started to creak open, and to Chad's disappointment, Luna quickly pulled her hand away and stood.

Gerry led Levi into the room. The blood had been cleaned off his head and face, and he was left with a butterfly bandage on his cheek and a patch of hair that had been shaved for his stitches.

"Levi is all ready to go," Gerry said. She handed Luna a white paper bag. "There's an energy potion, as well as one for pain, in there. If he needs more pain potion tomorrow, I've left a prescription in the bag. You can get it from Charming Herbals."

"I assume that means..." Luna cleared her throat. "All the tests were clear?"

Levi let out a small sigh and glanced away.

Luna winced. "Sorry."

He shrugged as if to say it didn't matter, but they all knew it did.

"Levi's bloodwork is completely normal," Gerry said. "Wake him up every couple of hours tonight. If the headache persists through tomorrow night, give me a call. Otherwise, come back in two weeks to get the stitches out."

"Two weeks?" Levi said.

Gerry patted his arm. "Don't worry. Taking them out is no big deal. Painless even."

Levi met Luna's gaze and then Chad's. It was obvious he was worried about where he was going to be in two weeks and not what he'd be doing.

"We'll make sure he's here," Luna said. "Thanks. We really appreciate you coming in so late to fix Levi up."

"Any time, Luna. You know that." She walked over to the door and held it open for them. "Go home and get some rest. I'll check in sometime tomorrow."

Luna ushered Levi out, and Chad paused to shake Healer Whipple's hand. "Thank you again. Can you send the bill to me at my stepmom's house? Barb Garber. I'll be taking care of it."

"Sure, Chad. I'll get admin to take care of it. Now get out of here. It's past my bedtime."

He grinned at her. "Mine, too."

Once Chad made it back out to the truck, they all climbed in and he drove to Luna's new place. He killed the engine, and for the first time since he'd gotten the call from Levi, he started to wonder what happened next. He was living in a one-bedroom apartment over his stepmom's garage. It wasn't that he couldn't afford to rent or buy a place in town. He just hadn't needed anything more... until now.

"I think Levi should stay here," Luna said abruptly.

"What?" Chad asked, surprised.

Luna nudged the teenager and whispered, "Why don't you go wait for me on my porch. I'll be right there."

Levi didn't hesitate. He pushed the door open, shuffled up to her front door, and leaned against the porch railing with his arms crossed over his chest.

"I know he called you tonight," Luna said softly as she turned to meet Chad's gaze. "But I get the feeling he could use a little mothering. Do you mind if he stays here?"

"What about when you go into work?" Chad asked, not wanting the kid to run the minute he was alone.

"I can take him with me, and you can take over after I work on your hand." She glanced over at him and let out a breath. "Wow. This feels like co-parenting or something."

Chad chuckled. "It does. But you're right. If I were him, I'd want to stay with you, too." The truth was he wanted to follow them both into her house right then and there. It had been a long day, and the idea of curling up next to her, holding her while they both slept, made him want to beg her to let him stay. "I'll meet you at the spa like you said and then take him to get some new clothes afterward. How's that sound?"

"Perfect. As long as he's on the same page." Luna pressed her hand to his cheek and leaned in, kissing the other one. "You're a good man, Chad. Thank you."

His skin tingled where her lips had brushed his skin. It took everything he had inside of him to not press his lips to hers and kiss her like he meant it. Instead, he squeezed her hand one last time and said, "There's nothing to thank me for. You were right there with me the entire time. Now go on. Levi's waiting. I'll see you both in the morning."

"Eight thirty. I'll bring the coffee and croissants." She grinned at him and hopped out. Chad waited until both of them disappeared into her house. Then he backed out of her driveway and went home to his lonely apartment.

CHAPTER 13

"*M*ake yourself at home," Luna said to Levi as she waved him into her newly rented house.

"This is your new place?" he asked, glancing at the lonely couch in the living room.

"Yep. It's a lot nicer than that apartment, isn't it?" She moved into the kitchen and went straight for the refrigerator. "Are you hungry? Want something to drink?" When he didn't answer, she glanced back and spotted him standing in the middle of the room, frozen like a deer in the headlights.

"Levi?" she called and walked over to him. "Are you all right?"

He turned to her with glassy eyes. "Why am I here?"

"Because you needed someone to care for you," she said softly and took him by the hand to lead him into the kitchen.

"But why would you do that?" He seemed genuinely perplexed and started glancing around. There was a nervousness to his darting eyes, and she wondered if he was planning his escape already.

"Listen, Levi," she started as she grabbed a glass from her

cabinet and filled it with filtered water from the fridge. As she pressed it into his hand, she continued, "First, I want to make it very clear that you are welcome to stay here for as long as you need a place to call home. I mean that. Okay?"

He gripped the glass so tightly his knuckles were starting to turn white.

"Nod if you understand me," she said gently.

He gave her one short nod.

"Good. Now as to why I'd offer help, well, as I told you yesterday, I was in foster care once. And to this day, I'm certain that the only reason I survived it is because someone looked after me and was there for me when I needed him. I'm only paying that favor forward."

His face hardened as he carefully put the glass on her counter. "So, this is all just some sort of karma payback for you. Do you think by helping a queer kid, you'll get your wings or something?"

She wanted to laugh but managed to keep her humor in check. "Wings? Now that's not something I'd considered. They seem pretty useless to be honest. I'd settle for something a little more mundane like a comfortable chair in my living room. Or maybe some upholstered bar stools for this counter."

He just blinked at her.

This time she did laugh. "Okay, I get it. Bad joke. Listen, I'm not looking for anything. All I want to do is help. I know what it's like to feel alone and scared. If I can change that for you, then that's enough for me. Okay?"

"And what about Chad? Why did he put his number in that fast food bag? What's his motive?" There was an edge to his questioning about Chad that hadn't been there before.

Luna frowned. "You know, Levi, I can't speak for him or why he wants to help you. I can only say that he's the person I was talking about who was there for me when I needed someone most. I trust him. And with my background, that doesn't come easy. No one expects it to come easy for you either. But I hope you'll try."

Skepticism was written all over his face. Who could blame him? This kid didn't know her or Chad. She couldn't comprehend the feelings he must've been processing. She just hoped that safe was one of them.

"Are you hungry?" she asked. "I don't have much, but there's some leftover pizza from last night in the fridge if you want it."

His eyes lit up, and she could see the longing in his expression.

"I'll heat it up for you," she said, moving past him to the fridge.

"You don't have to do that," he said. "I can do it."

"But I want to. Now go wash up. This will be ready in a couple of minutes." Once he disappeared into the downstairs half-bath, she set the timer on the stove and slid the remaining combination pizza onto a cookie sheet before popping it into the oven. With the pizza heating, she climbed the stairs and quickly changed the sheets on her bed and grabbed a spare sheet and couple of blankets for the couch. Then she jogged down the stairs and dumped her haul onto the couch.

"Is that for me?" Levi asked, coming over to help her make up the couch.

"Nope. Me. You're taking the bed. I've got the couch tonight."

"No way! I can't do that," he insisted. But the outburst made him wince, and he pressed his hand to the side of his head just below his stitched wound.

"You can, and you will," Luna said with a gentle smile. "I'll be fine down here. Besides, you'd be doing me a favor if you let me mother you a little bit."

His expression softened as some of the defensiveness disappeared from his wary eyes. "Okay," he said softly. "I think I can handle that."

"Good. Now let's get some of that pizza in you." She ushered him into the kitchen, retrieved the pizza from the oven, and gave him three of the four slices, keeping one for herself.

Since she still didn't have any bar stools or a table, they stood at the counter eating. Levi wolfed down two slices, and when he got to the third, he hesitated. "Are you sure you don't want this one?"

"I'm positive. In fact, you can have the rest of this one if you want. I'm full." She pushed the half-eaten slice over to him.

He shook his head. "No way. I'm not stealing your dinner. You can't be full off just half a slice."

"Trust me, I am," she said, patting her belly. "Chad and I had burgers before we got your call. If I eat anymore, I'll be uncomfortably stuffed."

Levi took a bite of his third slice, studying her. "I'm sorry I interrupted your date. I imagine this isn't how the evening was supposed to end."

"It wasn't a date," she said automatically, though as she heard herself say the words, she knew they were a lie. Why had she been so quick to deny the truth?

His eyebrows rose. "Really? Sure seems like you two are into each other."

Well, she was certainly into Chad, but she had no idea how he saw her. "I guess technically it was a date," she admitted. "I asked him out as a thank you for helping me move yesterday. As for being into each other, we're just friends."

An amused smile claimed his lips as he chuckled and shook his head slightly. His entire face lit up, and the heaviness that he carried with him seemed to melt away. He was beautiful, his brown eyes glinting, making her want to do anything to put that look on his face again. "I hate to be the one to break it to you, but you're not just friends. There are way too many sparks for that."

"There aren't any sparks," she lied, not wanting him to get the wrong idea… or let him encourage something that seemed unlikely.

He chuckled. "Yes, there are. Remember when we talked about me getting premonitions?"

"Yeah." Her heart did a major flip flop in her chest. What had he seen about them? And did she even want to know?

"I also see other things. Like actual sparks when two people who are into each other have any sort of physical contact. And when Chad touches you, there are fireworks."

They were probably just on her end, she decided. Because she had enough pent-up feelings for him to light up the sky. She just shrugged and then turned the focus away from her jumbled heart. "If you see that sort of thing, then it's official. You're definitely a spirit witch. What other abilities do you have besides the sparks and premonitions?"

His amusement vanished as his expression turned neutral, and it was his turn to shrug.

She laughed. "Okay, don't tell me. But I'm going to make it my mission to pry it out of you. Fair warning."

A faint smile reclaimed his lips. "You can try."

She chuckled. "Fair enough."

The conversation stilled as Levi finished the rest of the pizza. When he was done, he looked up at Luna, weariness etched around his eyes as he seemed to sway on his feet.

"Okay, visiting time is over. Time to get you to bed." She ushered him up the stairs and into her bedroom. "I've changed the sheets and laid out an old T-shirt and some sweatpants for you to sleep in. It's a good thing you're skinny or else I wouldn't have anything to loan you." She winked at him. "Don't worry, it's not anything too girly."

"It doesn't matter," he mumbled already sitting down on the bed.

She kneeled down and helped him out of his grungy shoes. The poor kid was in need of just about everything. "I don't have a spare toothbrush, but I left toothpaste and a fresh bar of soap in the bathroom. Use anything else you can find. We'll restock tomorrow. Gerry said you need to wait at least twenty-four hours before you can get your stitches wet, so be careful there. Okay?"

He nodded. "I can manage."

"I'm sure you can." She stood and walked to the door. "I'll be in after a few hours to wake you up. Healer's orders."

"All right." His voice was a rasp as he pushed himself off the bed and shuffled into the bathroom.

Luna wanted to wait and make sure he made it back to bed okay before she retreated downstairs, but she didn't want to make him feel like an invalid, so she grabbed a pair of pajamas from a box on the floor and forced herself back down to the living room. After a trip to the half bath to get ready for bed, she slipped beneath the covers of her makeshift bed on the couch and set the alarm on her phone. Exhaustion settled in her bones as she lay there wishing for sleep. But it never came. And when the alarm went off, she was still wide awake.

Without hesitation, Luna climbed the stairs and found the bedroom door slightly cracked open just the way she'd left it. She gave a short knock and heard a raspy, "Yeah?"

She pushed the door open and poked her head in. "Levi? You feeling all right?"

"Sure." He was curled on his side, the blanket pulled up to his neck, cocooned in the covers. Safe where she'd left him.

"Have you slept at all?" she asked as she made her way into the room. She sat on the edge of the bed next to him to get a look at his eyes. They were sleepy, but he didn't have a confused, dazed look. That was good.

"Some. I heard you coming up the stairs."

"You did?" She snorted. "And here I thought I was being quiet."

He closed his eyes, and a tiny shudder seemed to shake him. "I guess you could say I'm a light sleeper."

Dread curled in her belly. That shudder didn't have anything to do with his natural sleep patterns. This was a kid used to sleeping with one eye open. Her heart shattered all over again. She swallowed thickly. "I'll remember that. Any nausea? Dizziness?"

"No," he said sleepily. "Just a dull ache where the wound is."

"Okay. That's not so bad. It doesn't sound like you're suffering from a concussion, but I'll come and check on you in a few more hours anyway. Go back to sleep."

He mumbled something she didn't understand and stirred slightly before letting out a contented sigh.

Gah. That sound hit her straight in the heart. And this time when she curled under her blankets on the couch, she fell right to sleep.

CHAPTER 14

"*M*orning, sunshine," Luna said as Levi shuffled into her kitchen the next morning wearing his jeans from the day before and the vintage Rolling Stones T-shirt she'd left out for him the night before.

He glanced down at himself, plucking at the T-shirt. "I hope it's okay to borrow this. My shirt had blood on it."

"Of course," she said, sipping on a cup of coffee. "Keep it if you want. I have more where that came from."

"You do?" he stared at her cup, a look of longing on his face.

"Help yourself. There's more in the pot over there," she said, waving to the coffee maker on her counter. "I have a thing for second-hand stores and concert T-shirts. It's sort of my only weakness when it comes to spending money."

"That's cool." He found a mug and filled it with the dark roast.

"There's sugar in that container next to the pot and milk in the fridge if you want it," she added.

He doctored his coffee and leaned against the counter, studying his mug.

"Are you hungry? I don't have much, but there's bagels in the cupboard and cream cheese in the fridge. Or you can wait until we go to the café on the way to the spa. I always pick up something on the way to work."

"You work at a spa?" His gaze snapped up to meet hers.

"Yep. I'm a massage therapist."

"Oh."

There was an awkward silence, and not sure what else to do, Luna doctored a bagel for him whether he wanted it or not. "Here." She handed it to him. "You can still get something at the café later."

"Thanks." He took the bagel, but instead of devouring it like a normal teenager, he just held it as he bit down on his bottom lip.

"What is it, Levi? Do you need the pain reliever potion? You should probably eat before—"

"It's not that." He shook his head, and the tiny wince betrayed him. He might not be in agony, but he clearly wasn't one hundred percent. Not that she'd expected him to be. "I'm just wondering... um, what happens now?"

Luna glanced at the clock. "Well, in about ten minutes we'll leave for the café and then Chad will meet us at the spa. I'm going to do a little work on his hand, and then you two are going to go shopping to get you some basic necessities. After that..." She shrugged. "I guess we'll just play it by ear."

"You guys don't have to babysit me," he said, his voice rough. "I've been taking care of myself for a long time."

There was so much truth, so much pain, in his voice that Luna's eyes stung with unshed tears. She blinked them back and moved to stand right next to him, also leaning against the counter. "I'm sure that's true. But wouldn't it be nice if you had someone else to help you?"

106

He let out a bark of laughter. His next words were bitter and full of resentment. "That's for other people. People with normal families."

Luna reached over and grabbed his hand, holding on as tightly as she could. "I understand everything you're thinking and feeling right now. But remember when I told you you're welcome to stay here as long as you need?"

"Yeah," he said so quietly she barely heard him.

"That was absolutely the truth, but it also means as long as you *want* to as well. People like us, we don't have the luxury of depending on blood families, so we need to make our own."

"Is Chad your chosen family?" he asked.

The question took her aback at first. He'd just walked back into her life, and to consider him a close enough friend that she'd call him family seemed rushed or presumptuous. But the truth was he knew her better than anyone on the planet, and she knew without a doubt that if she needed him, he'd be there for her. And wasn't that what it meant to be family? She nodded. "Yes, I guess he is."

"You're lucky to have someone," he said and buried his face in the coffee mug.

"You're right about that. There's room for you in our circle, too, you know."

He tensed, and she decided not to push him further. She wanted so badly to put him at ease, to help heal what his family had broken inside of him, but that wasn't going to happen overnight. He needed time.

"Come on. Let's go find some pastries." She pushed off the counter. "I don't know about you, but I could use a big dose of sugar right about now."

Levi downed the rest of his coffee, and with the bagel still in his hand, he followed her out of the room.

"I'll be right back," Luna said. "I need to grab some socks." She left Levi in her living room and jogged up the stairs. Her bed had been made, and Levi's bloody T-shirt and the sweats she'd loaned him were folded and stacked in the corner. Damn, the kid was so careful to be respectful, just like she'd been anytime someone showed her any kindness at that age. Her heart simultaneously broke and melted at the same time. That was the moment she knew that as long as he wanted to, she was going to do everything in her power to make sure the state allowed him to stay with her.

After grabbing a fresh pair of socks, she stepped into her closet to look for a long sweater. It was often chilly in the morning in Keating Hollow, even in late spring. As she fished her sweater out of one of the boxes, she accidentally kicked over the one with her dirty clothes. Garments went everywhere, and she hastily shoved them back in their place.

When she was done, she spotted the envelope that had come for her a few days before at the spa. Oops. She'd shoved it in her jeans pocket and had promptly forgotten about it. She had no earthly clue who had written her or how'd they'd found her, but now she was intensely curious.

She ripped the envelope open and found a card with a big red heart on the front. That was strange. Flipping the card open, she read the first few lines:

Dear Luna,

My name is Gia McCormick, and I am your biological mother.

Luna sucked in a gasp and scanned the rest of the letter, her heart thundering against her ribcage. The letter was from a woman who was in recovery from a potions addiction and claimed to want to make amends for giving Luna up for adoption. There was a phone number at the bottom of the note, and it was signed, *Love, Mom.*

Emotion flooded Luna's system, and she was torn between screaming and crying. How dare this woman sign the note *Love, Mom*. Who the hell did she think she was? At the same time, Luna was overwhelmed with the possibility that her birth mother had reached out to her.

After Luna had turned eighteen and was released from juvy, she'd signed up on one of those registration sites that was designed to match adoptees with their birth parents. She hadn't found a match but had left her information in case either parent started looking for her. It wouldn't have been that hard for this woman to find her if she really was her birth mom.

But she hadn't counted on meeting a recovering addict. With Luna's history with her foster mother and the illegal potions the woman had made, Luna wasn't interested in being around anyone involved in that lifestyle. Though she had said she was in recovery. Still, there was a pit in Luna's stomach, and the idea of meeting this woman made her want to vomit.

But the note hadn't included any sort of information on why she'd given Luna up or why she wanted to meet her. All it said was she wanted to apologize because it was part of her program, not because she was sorry she gave her daughter up or because she wanted to get to know her. And that thought made Luna crumple the card in her hand. If Gia McCormick didn't actually care to know her daughter, then Luna wasn't going to make it easy for her. She shoved the crumpled card into her pocket and went downstairs to meet Levi.

CHAPTER 15

*T*here was something not quite right with Luna. Chad had noticed the moment he'd stepped into the spa reception area and spotted her frowning with her brows pinched together. And when she turned to him, her face was pale, and she looked almost haunted.

"Bad morning?" he asked.

"No," she said quickly as she glanced past him at someone else. "Why would you say that?"

"You seem... unsettled."

"I'm just tired," she said. "I'll perk up after the caffeine kicks in."

Chad turned and spotted Levi slumped down in one of the chairs, holding a cup from Incantation Café. "Hey, man. How's the head?"

"Better," Levi said, but he was studying Luna, and he looked troubled, too. Like he was worried about something.

That was all the confirmation he needed. There was definitely something up with Luna. Had something happened between them?

"Ready?" Luna asked him.

"Sure." Chad glanced back at Levi. "You okay here for a bit?"

"Yep."

"He's gonna be better than okay. I'm going to give him a manicure," Lena said and winked at him.

Levi snorted. "Oh, yeah? Who decided that?"

"I did." She swept out from behind the reception desk. "I'm taking pity on your poor cuticles. But don't worry, if you don't want polish, I won't force it on you."

"Do you have blue?" he asked.

"Honey, we've got every color you can think of. Follow me." She led him to a room just off the reception area. Before she slipped in behind him, she glanced back at Luna. "Take your time. I'm going to pamper him a little after everything he went through yesterday."

"Thank you," Luna said, her expression soft.

Hmm, Chad thought. Maybe whatever was bothering her wasn't about Levi at all. He hoped not.

"Come on," Luna said, leading him down the hallway to the massage rooms. Opening one of the doors for him, she asked, "How's your hand today?"

"Stiff." He held it out, trying to flex it, but he couldn't even straighten his fingers.

"Let's see if we can change that." Once they were inside, she said, "Go ahead and lie down on your back."

He quirked his eyebrow at her massage table. "Fully clothed?"

She rolled her eyes. "Yes. This is a hand job, not a full body massage."

"Hand job?" he asked, sputtering with amusement and no

small amount of lust. "That definitely seems like I should strip down."

"Stop." She laughed.

"That's better." He grinned at her, loving that his words had caused the moment of levity.

"Better than what?" She pulled a stool over to the massage table and took a seat.

"When I walked in, you looked like your dog had died. At first I thought something had happened between you and Levi, but now I think it's something else. Want to talk about it?"

She let out a heavy sigh, and the crease between her eyebrows reappeared as she frowned. "You're right, it's nothing to do with Levi. He's great. Scared and not sure if he can trust us yet, but that's to be expected."

Chad took his place on the massage table. "Understandable. So, what happened?"

Luna adjusted her chair and then took Chad's hand in hers. After drizzling some oil on her fingers, she started to work the muscles in his palm. "I got a letter from my birth mom," she blurted.

"Your birth mom?" he echoed, shocked. As far as Chad knew, Luna hadn't known who either of her birth parents were. When had that changed? "Since when have you been in touch with her?"

"I haven't." She swallowed. "This was the first contact."

"Wow." He wanted to reach out and squeeze her hand or put a soothing hand on her arm, but she was busy working the tension out of his fingers. Instead, he caught her gaze and held it. "What did the letter say, and why does it have you so freaked?"

She moved to the pad of his thumb and dug deep, making

him hiss, but she ignored his response and kept working the area. "Why do you think I'm freaked?"

"Maybe it was the fact that before you started talking with me, you were so pale you looked a little haunted."

She squeezed her eyes shut. "Really?"

"Yeah. I think Levi was worried, too," he said gently, wanting to make her aware that whatever she was going through might be affecting him, too.

"Damn. I don't want him to worry about anything other than getting better." She bit down on her bottom lip. "My mom is supposedly a recovering addict and wants to meet to make amends."

"I see." Chad knew it must've been a huge blow for Luna to find out the mother she'd always wanted to meet was an addict. With her background involving potions, including the relapses her foster mother had gone through, it would be hard for Luna to trust the recovery would stick. "And how do you feel about that? Do you want to meet her?"

"I did," she admitted, working his index finger. "But now? I don't think so. She's a potions addict, Chad. I just can't."

"You know you don't have to, right?" he asked, his voice gentle. "Just because she gave birth to you and reached out, that doesn't mean anything. She gave up the right to be in your life over twenty years ago. This is one hundred percent your call to make. Either choice is valid. Understand?"

Her eyes filled with tears as she nodded.

"Hey." He pulled his hand out of hers, sat up, and wrapped both arms around her, pulling her in for a hug. "You're okay, Luna. I promise."

"I know," she said into his shoulder. "But thank you for saying it."

"No need to thank me. That's what I'm here for." He pulled back and wiped one of her tears away.

"You're a good friend." Her smile was watery, but that lovely spark he loved so much had returned to her beautiful eyes.

Friend, he thought. He was glad she considered him one, but sitting there on her massage table, holding her, he was acutely aware that he wanted so much more than friendship. He wanted her. His gaze dropped to her pink lips and he worked to keep his breathing steady.

"Chad?"

His name on her lips almost made him shudder. But he held it together and raised his gaze to look her in the eye. "Yeah?"

"You should let me finish working on your hand."

"Right." With the spell broken, he laid back down and let her spin her magic.

Twenty minutes later, she placed a warm hand on his shoulder and in a quiet voice said, "All done. How do you feel?"

"Like I could take a nap right here," he said.

She laughed. "That's what you look like, too. But we have a teenager waiting for you to entertain him all day."

Chad groaned. "But this table is really comfortable."

"It had better be." She grabbed his good hand and tugged him into a sitting position. He knew it wasn't at all how she'd deal with a regular massage client, but this was an informal thing and he wasn't even paying for the massage. She waved a hand, shooing him toward the door. "Go on. I told Levi you'd take him shopping for some clothes and essentials. The poor kid has nothing with him."

"I'm on it," he said as he stood. "I'm also going to take him by Barb's garage. She asked me to take an inventory of her old furniture so she can start to get rid of it. I get first dibs, so if there is anything you need for your house, let me know. I'll haul it over for you."

"You can't do that, Chad. She said you get first dibs, not me," Luna said.

"Of course, I can. Mostly she just wants the stuff gone, and if I take it, she'll be thrilled, especially if it's for you."

"Why's that?" Luna asked.

"I dunno. She just likes you. She keeps saying I should ask you out." Oh, hell. What had he just said? The words had flown out of his mouth before he'd even given them any conscious thought.

Luna stared at him for a long moment, not saying a word.

"She's just trying to pair everyone up. Don't overthink it," Chad said.

"I'm not... overthinking it. But I do think you should ask me out." Her cheeks took on a rose flush as she glanced away. "Last night was fun... or it was until Levi called. I was just thinking that, um, well, maybe we should—"

Chad pressed a finger to her lips, stopping her. "Don't say it." He grinned, feeling all lit up inside. "It's my turn to do the asking."

Her smile reached her eyes, and she said, "Okay. I'm waiting."

He laughed. "Let me take you out Friday night. Dinner? Dancing? Maybe a moonlit walk on the beach this time?"

"The beach? You want to take me to the coast?"

"Sure, that's where the dancing is," he said easily. "It's a fundraiser actually. Cocktails, silent auctions, live music. Sounds stuffy and boring, but I promise it isn't. The Art Council puts it on, and all the proceeds go to supporting youth programs in Eureka."

"And you're involved how?" Luna asked.

"I've played piano for the organization before." He glanced down at his hand, realizing it didn't feel stiff for the first time in weeks. "Hey, my hand feels great by the way. Better than it has since the injury."

She beamed at him. "I might've used a little of my healing magic. I hope it's helping you heal and not just masking the pain."

"Me, too." He pressed his palm to her cheek. "Say yes to Friday."

"What about Levi?"

"He's a teenager. He can fend for himself for a few hours." Right? Chad pictured Levi hanging out by himself at Luna's house. Certainly, he was capable of taking care of himself, but what would happen when he was inside his own head? Kids who'd suffered trauma like he had were often unpredictable. "We'll work something out. I'll ask Candy if any of the teenagers in town have something going on."

Candy was Hanna's cousin and worked part time at the café. She was an outgoing, friendly girl, who likely would befriend Levi on her own. It was just her nature. Chad would make sure they ran into each other while he and Levi were out running errands.

"That would be good," Luna said, nodding. "I know he's old enough that he doesn't need any sort of babysitter, obviously, and I don't want him to feel like we think he does, but I worry. I know what I was like when I felt alone at that age. It wasn't pretty."

"He probably needs someone to talk to," Chad said.

"Yep. I agree." She glanced at the door. "But first I'm going to make an appointment with Lorna White to find out what we can and can't do for Levi."

"Good. The sooner the better." Lorna White was Keating

Hollow's resident attorney. Chad just hoped she had decent experience with family law. "Let me know if you want me to go with you."

"I will." She raised her gaze to his. "Now, about Friday…"

"Yeah?" he asked, nearly holding his breath. *Say yes*, he thought. *Let me hold you close while we dance the night away.*

"The answer is yes. What time will you pick me up?"

Happiness flooded his chest, and this time when he looked down at her, he couldn't resist. He leaned in and brushed his lips over hers. She was so soft, so sweet, so *his*.

Gods. He'd barely touched her and was already claiming her. He pulled back. "It's a date. Let me know any furniture you're looking for and I'll check Barb's storage. I assume you could use another bed for Levi?" He paused and studied her. "Are you sure you're good with him moving in indefinitely?"

Her head bobbed. "More than sure."

"That's what I thought, but I didn't want to assume. Okay, a bed for Levi. Anything else?"

She chuckled. "Just about everything else, Chad. You've seen what little I have. But most important is a second bed, barstools or a kitchen table and chairs, and a couple of dressers."

Chad tapped her list into his phone. "That's a good start. I'll text you pictures of what we find, and you can say yeah or nay. Cool?"

"More than cool." She looked up at him with wonder in her eyes, and he recalled it was the same look she'd had when he'd told her she could have his spare bedroom when she turned eighteen. Surprise, hope, trust, it was all right there at the surface, and he loved that he'd been the one responsible for putting that look in her eyes.

"Good." He couldn't resist. He leaned down and kissed her

LOVE OF THE WITCH

again. This time he slipped his tongue past her lips and tasted honey. "Yum. Perfect."

She leaned into him, deepening the kiss and letting out a tiny moan of appreciation.

Jeez. If she did that again, he was going to pick her up and toss her on her massage table. Reluctantly, he pulled away. "You probably have clients coming soon."

"Ten minutes," she confirmed.

"Right. Text ya later."

"You better," she said and opened the door for him.

After he was gone, Luna pulled the wrinkled card out of her pocket and stared at the number. Then she walked over to the phone and dialed.

CHAPTER 16

*C*had parked his truck in front of Incantation Café. "You hungry?" he asked Levi.

The teenager shrugged.

What the hell did that mean. "I don't speak teenager. Want to elaborate?"

Levi mumbled something as he turned his head and looked out the window.

Chad decided he'd be annoyed if he wasn't so amused. He could just hear his mother telling him he was trying her patience. "I didn't catch that. Want to try again?"

"I don't have money," he barked out.

"Ah. I see. Well, the good news is you don't need any. It's on me today." Chad jerked his head toward the café. "You can buy some other time."

Levi let out an incredulous huff of laughter. "With what, dude?"

Chad shrugged. "You'll get back in school and maybe get a job. I'm in no hurry. Now let's get food and then head to the store for essentials." Without waiting for an answer, Chad jumped out of the truck and strode into the café. A few moments later, Levi joined him.

Candy appeared from the back room, her dark hair pulled up into a thick, curly ponytail. She took one look at Levi and gave him a sassy smile. "Well, hello there. You're new in town."

Levi turned his attention to her and nodded slightly. Candy was a pretty girl with flawless bronze skin, big dark eyes, and a trim athletic body. Chad figured any teen boy would go loopy for her. But Levi didn't seem interested in that way. Instead he leaned his hip against the counter and said, "Great makeup."

She beamed, her smile lighting up the room. "Thank you. I'm a makeup video junky. All that time must be paying off. Love that shade of blue polish. What's it called?"

He shrugged. "No idea. Lena over at the spa did them."

Candy rubbed her hands together in excitement. "Perfect. I'll ask her. Now what can I get you two?"

She took their orders and said she'd bring everything out when it was ready.

"So. Candy," Chad said to Levi as they sat down. "What do you think?"

Levi gave him a flat stare. Then his expression turned wary as he said, "I'm not into girls."

"Right," Chad said quickly, wanting to put him at ease. He'd figured that out pretty quickly while watching their exchange. "I meant do you think she'd be friend material?"

"Dude," Levi said, sounding annoyed. "Why are you trying to fix me up with someone I met a half-second ago?"

Chad's face warmed. Then he laughed. Levi wasn't a toddler. He didn't need anyone to facilitate playdates for him. Honesty is the best policy, right? It was worth a try. "The thing is I want to take Luna out on a date on Friday. And while she knows you can take care of yourself, she's a little

hesitant about leaving you alone so soon since your...
accident."

"You mean so soon since my uncle beat the crap out of me,"
he said, careful to keep his tone neutral.

"Yeah. That. Sorry, man." Chad ran a hand through his hair.
"She'd probably just feel better if you had some friends to hang
out with. That's all."

"Friends," Levi muttered. "That's not... never mind."

Chad tilted his head. "Friends aren't what?"

Levi blew out a breath, and Chad could almost see the
moment when the kid came to the same realization Chad had
only moments before. Sometimes it was just easier to tell the
truth. "I've only had one friend, my best friend, and when his
parents found out I was gay a couple of years ago, that was it.
Cut off."

Chad's stomach roiled. There wasn't much in this world he
hated more than bigotry. Especially when it was unloaded on
kids. "That's really messed up. I'm sorry that happened."

"Me, too." He glanced out the window.

Son of a... Chad didn't know what to do with that. All signs
pointed to Levi being a decent kid with a kind heart. He
wanted to pull the kid into a giant hug and promise that life
would get better. That it wouldn't always be that bad. But who
was he to make any such claim? He had no idea what the future
held for him past the next few days or weeks. "I know it's
cheesy and I'm an old-dad type, but you can count me as a
friend, Levi."

The kid flicked his gaze back to him. "I hope you didn't
mean that in a creepy way."

Chad jerked back, startled by the comment. Then he
squeezed his eyes shut and shook his head. "Gods, Levi. No."

"Then why?" Levi demanded. "I don't get it. You and Luna,

you two are like saviors who just flew down from heaven, if there is such a place. But I don't deserve that. I'm not special. Why are you putting yourselves out like this unless you want something from me?"

Chad sat back with his arms crossed over his chest, studying him. "I'm here because when I was slightly younger than you, my step dad was an abusive asshole, and I didn't feel like I had anyone to turn to for help. I was terrorized for longer than I care to talk about, and I often wonder what might have been different if I'd told just one person. One adult who might know what to do or say to change things for me. Our situations are different, Levi, but you needed help and it makes me feel good to offer that help. No kid should be alone and scared. So the reason I want to help you is because my fourteen-year-old self wished so badly there was someone I could have turned to back then. I'm doing it for the kid I used to be. Or at least I was at first. Now I'm doing it because I like you. You're a cool kid who deserves a break. If you want to know Luna's reasons, you'll have to ask her."

"I already did," he said, his eyes wide. "She said something very similar. Something about paying it forward."

Interesting. This kid obviously didn't let anyone in easily. Who could blame him? Chad just hoped he'd managed to strip back at least one of Levi's many shields. They'd need to barrel through most of them if Levi was ever going to heal after the rejection he'd already received in his young life.

"Brunch is served," Candy said in a sing-song voice as she placed the plates on the table. "I'll be back in a second. Need to get your drinks. Sorry for making you wait."

Chad watched Levi as he watched her saunter away.

"She really is hot," Levi said almost wistfully.

"I thought you said girls weren't your thing?" Chad challenged.

He laughed. "They aren't. But dang, I can enjoy the view of a sexy woman, can't I?"

"Fair enough," Chad said.

They were still chuckling when Candy returned with their drinks. Then Levi surprised Chad when he asked Candy, "Hey. Is there anything interesting happening in this town on Friday night? Any teen get-togethers or hangouts I should know about?"

"Hmm, nothing official. But if you're looking for a hangout partner, I'm free. Just friends though. I've got a boyfriend."

Levi grinned at her. "Is he hot?"

Her eyes crinkled with amusement. "Heck, yeah. Why?"

"I'm just wondering if he has an available brother," he said with a shrug.

Candy barked out a laugh. "No, however..." She eyed him up and down. "Yeah, okay. Come out with us on Friday night. There's someone you need to meet."

"Oh, no. Not a set up." Levi shook his head, his face turning a dark shade of red. "I'm not great in those situations."

"Nerves," she says nodding. "I get it. But don't worry. This will be a group thing." She pulled her phone out of her pocket. "What's your number? I'll text you the details."

Levi's mouth opened then closed as he shook his head. "My phone died recently. Haven't had a chance to get a new one yet," he muttered.

"Oh. Well, let me give you my number and you can text me later," she said without hesitation. She retreated back to the counter, scribbled a number, and when she returned, she handed it to Levi.

"Yeah, okay," he said, tucking it into his jeans pocket, but he looked out the window with a defeated expression on his face.

Candy glanced at Chad, a concerned look on her face, seeming to ask, *What did I say?*

Chad gave her a slight shake of his head, not sure how to answer. He could guess what Levi was thinking. He wouldn't have a phone. He wouldn't have much of anything, and at the moment he didn't even have a change of clothes.

"It's nice to meet you, Levi," Candy said. When he glanced at her, she added, "It's always nice to meet cute, interesting boys. See you Friday."

"Thanks, you too." He cleared his throat. "Looking forward to it."

She waved and went back behind the counter to deal with the line forming.

CHAD LED Levi down the sidewalk of the strip mall. "Any stores look promising?"

They'd ended up in Eureka since Keating Hollow didn't exactly have clothing stores that catered to moody teens. Chad pointed to the Old Navy store. "How about that one. Or the Gap. They have good jeans, right?"

Levi rolled his eyes. "I can't shop at either of those places."

"And why not?" Chad crossed his arms over his chest, getting really tired of the money excuse. Levi didn't want to do anything that cost money. It was obvious he didn't want to take advantage or owe anyone anything.

"I just…" Levi jammed his hands into his front pockets.

"Just what?"

"Can we go to a second-hand shop? Like the Buffalo Exchange?" Levi asked.

"Vintage?" Chad's interest perked right up. "Yeah. Let's do that."

Once they were in the secondhand shop, Chad was able to convince Levi to get enough clothing to last at least a week. When Levi kept insisting he needed to find a way to pay him back, Chad said, "Don't worry about it, man. You can help me get the store set up. If you want to work there, I'll take it out of your pay."

Levi turned and stared at him. "What?"

"I'm opening a music store in Keating Hollow. I'll need someone to help me with painting and store set up. You game?"

"Hell, yeah!"

"Good." Chad slipped his arm around the kid's shoulders and led him up to the front counter. "Let's get this stuff and then we'll hit Target for the rest of your necessities before we head back to town and raid Barb's storage. With any luck, we'll have everything moved into Luna's house before she gets off work."

Levi's elated expression faded, and he glanced away again.

Chad swallowed a frustrated sigh. What now? The furniture was free. Even though he fully expected the kid to dodge his question, he straight out asked, "Levi, what's going on?"

To his surprise, Levi turned worried eyes on him and said, "I think she's changed her mind."

"About what?"

"About me staying there. This morning she got really weird and quiet, and I... I shouldn't stay long."

Chad grabbed Levi's arm and squeezed lightly. "That's not

at all the truth, Levi. She got some news this morning she wasn't expecting, and it has nothing to do with you. Trust me. If you leave because of anything she said this morning, she'll be gutted. She's not going to let you back out on the streets if she has anything to say about it. If you don't want to stay in Keating Hollow, that's one thing. We'll help you find a safe place—"

"I don't want to leave," he said quickly, looking away as his eyes turned glassy.

Chad let out a relieved breath. "Good. That's good." He let go of Levi's arm and took a step back. "Ready to stroll the personal hygiene aisle of Target?"

Levi ran a hand through his hair, making it stand up in messy clumps. He grimaced and patted it back down. "More than ready."

Chad could only imagine. He'd obviously showered since Chad had seen him the night before, but Luna likely didn't have a spare deodorant or tooth brush or anything else he needed lying around. "Let's do it then."

It was late in the afternoon when Chad and Levi finished putting together the bed they'd hauled over to Luna's from Barb's storage. It was a double bed with a slightly lumpy mattress, but Levi was beaming as he stared down at the piece of furniture. "Do you know how long it's been since I've had my own bed to sleep in?"

"About twelve hours?" Chad teased. "Did Luna give you hers last night?" After the run to Target, Levi had finally relaxed and spent the rest of the day smiling. It was good to see him accepting the help Chad and Luna so desperately wanted to give him.

Levi rolled his eyes. "Besides that. I only took it because my head was killing me and arguing with Luna was making me nauseous."

"Of course," Chad said nodding. "Sometimes it's better to just let the women have their way. I get it." He winked. "So, how long?"

"Nine or ten years," Levi said with a shrug. "I acquired four step siblings after my dad got remarried. All of them younger than me. They gave my bed to my oldest sister and I got a couch." His eyes flashed with anger as he added, "They were supposed to buy me a new bed, but as it turned out, the stepmonster's children always needed something else more. And then when they suspected I was gay… well, I was probably lucky they didn't kick me out sooner."

"Damn, Levi. That's brutal. I'm sorry, man." Chad clapped him on the shoulder.

"Yeah. It was," he said simply. Then he looked down at the bed again and beamed. "But thanks to you and Barb, I'm going to enjoy the heck out of this."

"Yes, you will," Luna said, striding into the room. "But put this on top before you secure the sheets. It will keep your back from aching." She tossed a foam bed topper on the mattress and then rushed out, only to return a moment later with sheets, two blankets, and a couple of pillows.

Staring at the bedding, Levi asked, "Where did this stuff come from?"

Luna shrugged. "The bedroom fairy."

Levi's eyes sparkled with amusement as he sputtered, "Bedroom fairy? Do I get one of those too? Is he my type?" As soon as the words flew out of his mouth, he let out a gasp and clasped his hand over his mouth as he mumbled, "Sorry."

Luna just laughed. "If there was such a thing as a bedroom fairy, I'd be first in line for one."

Levi's eyes were wide with surprise as he gaped at her. Chad turned his attention to her, his body temperature rising as he imagined crawling onto her bed and covering her body with his own. *Holy hell,* he thought as he glanced away. *Not now, dude. Not now.*

CHAPTER 17

*L*una didn't miss the look Chad was giving her. And her body responded instantly with a flutter of her heart, followed by tingles dancing over her skin. He hadn't even touched her, and yet, she felt like she could already feel his fingertips gliding over her skin.

"Wow. I feel like a third wheel. I'll just head downstairs while you two, ah, do whatever it is you're going to do," Levi said with a snicker and rushed out of the room.

Luna watched him go, horrified. Her face heated and she averted her gaze.

Chad chuckled.

"What's so funny?" she asked him with narrowed eyes.

"Us." He reached out and lightly grabbed her hand, tugging her closer to him. "We can keep dancing around this, or we can acknowledge that we're both goners."

She blinked up at him. "I don't know what you're talking about. We should—"

Chad placed his fingers over her lips, stopping her words. "Yes, you do." Instead of pulling his hand away, he gently ran his thumb over her bottom lip. "Do you have any idea how much I want to kiss you right now?"

Luna's breath caught. She wanted more than anything to lean into him and taste him again. The kiss they'd shared back at the spa had stayed with her all day. She'd be lying if she pretended that she didn't want him, too. She let out a small sigh and leaned in, whispering, "We shouldn't be doing this right now."

"Probably not," he agreed, but he cupped her cheeks with both hands and brushed his lips over hers. "But I've been wanting to do this since that first day I saw you sitting at the bar in the brewpub."

She made an appreciative noise and leaned into the kiss, unwilling to tell him exactly how long she'd wanted him. He tasted of chocolate and coffee and home. Her arms went around his solid frame, and she wondered if she'd ever felt as right as she did in that moment. She was exactly where she was supposed to be with the only man she'd ever loved.

Life felt just about perfect.

She stiffened and then pulled back, startled and more than a little freaked. Perfect wasn't good. Perfect meant that likely the shit was about to hit the fan. Perfect was a fleeting moment, and she was sure her bubble was about to burst.

"What just happened?" he asked, studying her face, his eyes searching. "Where'd you go?"

"Back to reality. Listen, Chad. There's a sixteen-year old boy downstairs. I know you told me you two had a good day and he's doing fine, but that kind of trauma, it doesn't just disappear. I need to go make dinner and talk to him about the next steps. Not stay up here, making out with you." Her gaze dropped to his lips, and she had to force herself to look away. "Are you done in here?"

"Uh, yeah." He ran a hand through his light hair and blew out a breath. Then his easy smile was back as he said, "Okay. You're right about that. Let's go make dinner."

Her heart dropped as disappointment set in. She hadn't expected him to agree so easily. Or maybe she just hoped he wouldn't. Too late. She'd put on the brakes and he'd respected her decision. Of course, he had. Pushing wasn't his style.

"Right." She spun on her heel and started for the door.

"Luna?"

"Yeah?" she glanced over her shoulder.

"We'll revisit this Friday after I pick you up for our date." He gave her a sexy half smile before striding past her and down the stairs.

Cocky bastard, she thought, but as she made her way down to the kitchen, she couldn't help the silly grin on her face or the butterflies that had taken up residence in her stomach. He wanted her, and he was making sure she knew it. She just hoped she wasn't jumping off the deep end without a life preserver.

She found Levi in the kitchen chopping a bell pepper. He'd already worked his way through an onion and a bag of carrots she'd brought home from the grocery store. When she glanced past him, she spotted a bowl of cut up chicken breasts. "Hey," she said, grinning at him. "Looks like you know your way around a kitchen."

He shrugged. "I'm not a gourmet cook or anything, but I know stir fry ingredients when I see them."

"You want some help or—"

"I got it," he said, waving a hand. But then he paused, that worried look in his eyes again. "Unless you wanted to do the cooking. I'm just so used to fending for myself that I didn't think to ask."

"Levi, you can cook anything you want at any time. You don't need to ask. Especially if you're cooking us dinner."

Relief washed over him, and his shoulders relaxed. "Okay. Cool. I like to cook. I'm happy to do that whenever you want."

"The job is yours," she said with a wide smile. The fact that he'd taken it upon himself to just start dinner for them made Luna's heart squeeze. Guh. He was such a sweet kid. She couldn't help wondering again for the twentieth time how he'd ended up homeless. Since he had it all under control, she sat on the newly acquired stool across from him and clasped her hands together. "Can we talk a minute?"

He paused, holding the knife above the red pepper. "About what?"

Luna sucked in a breath, not wanting to upset him, but if he was going to stay, she needed to find a way to make it official. She didn't want him to settle in and get attached, and then get pulled out of her home for any number of preventable reasons. "I want to talk to a lawyer about where we go from here, and I'm going to need some information first."

"A lawyer?" His face was pinched as if he was worried.

"Yes, someone who can help us figure out how you can legally stay here. I need to find out how I can become your legal guardian so we can get you back in school and your uncle can't just come and order you back into your old situation. I didn't mean to pry earlier, but I overheard you say your dad kicked you out when I was coming upstairs a few minutes ago. Is there any reason to believe he might want you to come back now that there's been some distance?"

His face paled, and he blinked rapidly, clearing the tears that appeared suddenly. "No. He's not interested in a... relationship with me."

Luna longed to wrap him in her arms and somehow just hold on until all of his wounds were healed. But she knew that wouldn't happen in one night. Probably not even a lifetime, but she was up for trying. "Okay. I'm sorry to hear that for your sake, but hopefully it means it will be easier to get all the legal stuff in place for you to stay here. What do you say about meeting with a lawyer so that your uncle can't claim a legal right as a guardian?"

A visible shudder ran though him as undeniable fear flashed in his big brown eyes. He glanced around as if looking to see if his uncle was already in Luna's house demanding that Levi get back to Eureka. "No. I won't go with him. Not ever again. I won't," he insisted.

Luna reached across the counter and gently squeezed his hand. "That's what I want to avoid. Trust me, Levi, I don't want you in that situation. That's why I want to consult someone. So you're protected."

"But what…" He swallowed hard and his eyes turned glassy with unshed tears again.

Luna was silent as she waited for him to find his courage to ask whatever it was that he was thinking.

"Um, what if the lawyer has to contact someone?" He averted his gaze, and his voice was barely a whisper as he asked, "Like… Child Protective Services?"

An ache formed in Luna's gut. That was always a possibility. But she couldn't just have a kid living with her without getting some sort of legal protection for both of them. "Then I'll do whatever it takes to make sure they let you stay here. Which brings me to my next question."

He dropped his chin to his chest and asked, "What?"

"How do you feel about reporting your uncle? I know the deputy sheriff here in town. You can trust him."

Levi's head snapped up, and his expression was hard. "No. No cops."

Luna suppressed a sigh. She figured he wouldn't trust the local law enforcement. She hadn't either at his age. All of her interactions with cops up until that point had ended with her in another crappy foster home or hassled just for being an aimless teen out too late in the city who wasn't willing to go home. It had taken her a while to realize that most of them actually wanted to help but were confined by their jobs concerning how much they could do. Levi had no way of knowing that Drew Baker, Keating Hollow's deputy, was a good man. Drew would never do anything to put Levi back in danger. But Luna wasn't about to break Levi's trust. "Okay. No reports for now. But keep in mind that the sooner you report the incident, the better. Child Protective Services won't send you back to your uncle with a criminal complaint against him."

A single tear ran down Levi's cheek as he slowly shook his head. "I just want to disappear."

Luna's heart twisted. She'd been there more times than she could count. "I know, sweetie. I really do. And it kills me that I can't make any promises about the outcome of this. The only thing I can promise is that I will always be here and will do my damnedest to not let you down."

A sob got caught in his throat as he tried to suck in a breath.

That was it. That was the moment Luna lost her heart to the kid. She slid off the stool and rounded the counter, her arms stretched out wide.

Levi turned into her, burying his head in her shoulder, and she wrapped her arms around him, holding him tight.

"We'll find a way through this. Whatever it takes, I'm here for it. Understand?"

He nodded, his tears soaking into her T-shirt.

They stood together in the kitchen, Luna whispering soothing words to him while she just held on, almost as if she was physically trying to hold him together.

Footsteps sounded behind her, and she wasn't at all surprised when Chad wrapped his arms around both of them and said, "Count me in. Whatever we need to do, I'm game."

Levi let out a choked chuckle. "You two are crazy."

Chad let go as Luna pulled back and released Levi so that she could look him in the eye. "You know, you're probably right. But it's a good crazy. I'm just crazy enough to move to a small town where I don't know anyone and build a life for myself. One that now includes a teenager."

"And a piano teacher," Chad added with a grin.

She glanced at him, one eyebrow raised in question.

"What? You didn't think you were getting rid of me now that I've found you again, did you?" he asked.

"No. I just… never mind." She shook her head slightly, wondering if she was getting in too deep with him. The thought almost made her laugh. *Getting?* She was already there. She always had been.

"What is it, Luna?" he asked, studying her.

"Nothing. I guess I'm just still getting used to having you back in my life."

His grin was lopsided as he winked at her, making her flush.

Levi let out a loud sigh as he went back to dealing with the stir fry.

"What is it, Levi?" Luna asked.

His eyes were full of affection as he said, "You two are relationship goals."

"Um, we're just friends," Luna insisted. Friends who'd been on the verge of making out upstairs.

"You just keep telling yourself that," Levi said, turning to the stove and pouring olive oil into a pan.

Chad placed his hand on the small of her back and kissed her on the cheek. "Listen to the kid. I think he knows what he's talking about."

She rolled her eyes but couldn't help grinning up at him.

They stared at each other for a long moment. Finally, Chad stepped back and pulled a phone out of his pocket. He turned to Levi. "Hey, do you still have Candy's number?"

"Yeah. Why?"

"Hand it over," Chad said, punching a number into the phone to unlock it.

Levi glanced over his shoulder at Chad. "Why?"

Chad held his hand out. "Because, I need to text her something."

Reluctantly, Levi handed him the number. "You're not going to embarrass me or anything, are you?"

Chad laughed. "Of course not."

"Why is that not reassuring?" Levi muttered.

Luna chuckled as she looked over Chad's shoulder. The text read:

Hey Candy, got a new phone today. Here's the number. Text me about Friday. Levi.

He hit send and then held the phone out to Levi. "Here. I picked this up for you today."

Levi looked back at him again and froze, his eyes locked on the iPhone.

Chad moved forward still holding out the phone. "Please don't fight me on this. You need a phone. We need a way to get in touch with you, and I've already activated it on my contract.

There's no turning it off now, and I can't use two phones, so you might as well."

A lump formed in Luna's throat. Was this really happening? Had Chad really taken it upon himself to get Levi a phone? Of course he had. She didn't really know why she was so surprised. He'd always been generous. "Take it, Levi. It's all right, I promise."

Levi's breath caught as he tentatively reached a hand out, gingerly taking the phone from Chad. "I still don't understand why you're being so kind to me."

"You'll get it one day," Chad said. "When you're older and you realize you're in a position where you can help someone, I'm certain you will. Your reasons won't be exactly the same as mine, but they'll be close enough."

Levi studied the phone with wide-eyed wonder. "Thanks, man."

Chad clapped him on the back. "You're welcome. The plan is unlimited, so don't worry about data usage. Sound good?"

"Sounds fantastic." Levi abandoned his dinner and threw his arms around Chad, hugging him tightly. "Thank you." He laughed again. "I'll be working for you for five years just to pay you back. Maybe by then I'll have some pocket change."

"You're not paying me for the phone, kid. I did that for me and Luna, so we won't worry about not being able to get in touch with you. But lucky you, you now have access to all the things teenagers do that happens to be online. Just don't be running up game charges or anything. Any extras that show up in the bill are definitely yours."

"Got it," Levi said and shoved the phone into his pocket. "Don't worry. I'm not a gamer."

Chad just nodded and then wandered over to the couch

while Luna tilted her head and eyed Levi. "You have plans on Friday? Did I hear that right?"

"Sure. The Chadster over there is taking you out, so I made a new friend. She invited me out Friday, and I'm going to go and see who else I can meet in this town."

"Good plan. You sound like a kid who is eager to get his life rolling again," Luna said.

"I guess I am."

"Does that mean you're okay if I meet with the lawyer?" she asked.

He hesitated, his face pinched. Then he closed his eyes and nodded. "Just... can you tell me everything she says?"

"Of course. In fact, why don't you come with me? I'll make an appointment for tomorrow afternoon. Sound okay?"

"Yeah. Okay." He blinked his glassy eyes and turned back to finish the stir fry.

CHAPTER 18

*L*orna White sat at her desk, her straight, long gray hair framing her angular face. Blue eyes peered at Luna as the attorney pressed her fingertips together in thought.

Luna glanced over at Levi. The kid was hunched down in his armchair, worrying the hem of the Nirvana T-shirt he was wearing. She wanted to reach over and squeeze his hand but knew the gesture would be unwelcome right at that moment. Levi had been curling in on himself ever since they'd walked into the woman's office.

"Levi," the attorney said. "Do you know of any formal custody agreements between your father and your uncle? Any paperwork that might be on record with the state?"

"No. My father kicked me out and I ended up on my uncle's doorstep two days later. I'm not sure my dad even knows I was there."

"So no email communication or texts of any kind?" she pressed.

Levi shrugged. "It's possible I guess, but they aren't close. I doubt it."

"Okay." She leaned forward and met Luna's gaze. "Instead of getting Child Protective Services involved—"

Levi winced.

Lorna gave him a sympathetic grimace. "Sorry. I know it sounds awful, and I want to avoid that if at all possible. Understand?"

Levi gave her a nod but sank even deeper into the chair. Luna thought that if he went even another inch, he might just slide right off the thing.

"As I was saying," Lorna said to Luna, "the best course of action is to get Levi's father to sign a document giving you physical custody. No courts, no CPS, no red tape." She turned her attention to Levi. "Do you think he'd be willing to do something like that?"

"As long as it doesn't cost him any money," Levi blurted.

It was Luna's turn to wince. The fact that Levi's father cared so little for his own son wasn't a surprise, but that didn't make it hurt Levi any less. And even though he was speaking matter-of-factly, Luna knew there was no way he wasn't affected. She sucked in a deep breath and said, "It won't."

The attorney nodded. They'd already discussed that Luna wasn't interested in asking for money from the man, and any fees that were incurred during the process, she'd pay.

"Then I'm sure he won't care." Levi turned his head, avoiding everyone's gaze.

"And your mother? Where is she?" Lorna asked.

"She died when I was really little," Levi muttered. "Overdose."

Luna wanted to cry for him but forced herself to stay calm.

She knew from experience that pity usually made everything worse.

"I'm sorry to hear that," Lorna said. "Okay, one last question for you, Levi."

The teenager looked up at her, his mouth stretched into a thin line.

"Do you want to stay with Luna? Do you want me to pursue this avenue?"

He let out a humorless laugh as he glanced at Luna. "Do you really expect me to say no with her sitting right here?"

Luna held Levi's gaze, searching for his truth. There was a mixture of emotion in his eyes: sadness, wariness, frustration, dejection, and maybe even a little bit of hope.

"You can be honest with me, Levi," Luna said. "I hope you know that. I only want what's best for you at this point. If staying with me isn't the right fit, I'll help you figure out where you should be." Though, honestly, she'd already fallen for the kid. If he bailed out, she'd be heartbroken. Still, she'd do what was needed to make sure he was safe.

The tears were back in Levi's eyes as he tore his gaze away from Luna. He focused on Lorna and said, "I want to stay with Luna."

Relief rushed through Luna, and she let out the breath she'd been holding.

"Good. I think that's an excellent decision," the attorney said. She beamed at Levi as she passed him some forms. "If you fill this out, we can get in touch with your father and get the paperwork moving."

"I⊤ can't be that easy," Levi said as they left the attorney's office and stepped out onto the cobbled sidewalk.

"He still has to sign the paperwork," Luna said, not wanting him to think this was just a formality. It could be, though, if his father really didn't care one way or another. But if he was feeling vindictive or uncharitable for any reason, he could just as easily tell Lorna White to shove the paperwork into the nearest orifice.

"He will. As long as my stepmonster doesn't want me there, he'll do the easiest thing he can to get rid of me. I think this will work."

"Come here." She draped an arm around his shoulders. "You understand that I want you here with me, right?" Luna stopped suddenly and turned him so that he was forced to look her in the eye. "That you are in no way disposable?"

Tears welled in his eyes and rolled silently down his cheeks as he shook his head, pain etching his face.

"Levi," she whispered and pulled him into a hug, and again she said, "You are not disposable."

He let out a sob and clung to her.

"Some people in this world don't know how to love. I'm not one of them," she added, vowing to never let this kid down. They stood on the street for a few more beats until Levi pulled away and wiped at his eyes. Luna squeezed his arm. "Come on. Chad is waiting for you at the pub."

"What about you?" he asked, his voice still nasally from his tears.

"I… well, I kind of have my own parent crisis to deal with." She let out a nervous chuckle. "It appears my birth mom wants to speak to me. I agreed to meet her in Eureka this evening."

Levi squinted at her. Then he shook his head. "You shouldn't go alone."

"Why?" she asked as she stepped up to her car and pulled the door open.

He frowned, his eyebrows pinching together in a troubled expression. "I'm picking up on something... it feels tumultuous. Chaotic even."

She just shrugged. "I imagine everyone feels like that the first time they meet their birth mother."

"That's not—"

"Come on. Get in. You can continue to tell me how awful it's going to be while I drive you to the pub."

He rolled his eyes but climbed into the car.

Luna jammed the key into the ignition and cranked. Nothing happened. She tried again. Nothing at all. "Oh, come on. Not now."

"Seems like a battery problem," Levi said, already getting out of the car. He rounded the front of the vehicle and indicated that Luna should pop the hood. She did as he asked, even though she had no earthly idea if he had a clue what he was doing.

She sent Chad a text to let him know what was going on and then climbed out of the car to join Levi.

"Battery?" she asked.

"Maybe. Could be your alternator, too. We need to try to jump it." Levi walked away from the car and spoke to an older couple who'd just pulled into the space beside them.

It didn't take long for the gray-haired gentleman to produce some jumper cables. They got everything set up fairly quickly and then sent Luna back to the driver's seat. When she turned the engine over, there wasn't even a clicking noise. She let out a frustrated groan.

"Sorry that didn't work. Looks like you'll need to take it to the shop." The man put the cables away, and Luna shook his hand, thanking him.

"Hey," Chad said from somewhere behind her.

She swung around, looking for his handsome face, and found him walking swiftly toward her. "No luck?"

She shook her head. "Jumping didn't help. Not sure what the problem is."

Chad pulled his phone out of his pocket and dialed. "I'll get a tow truck to take care of it, and then I'll take you to Eureka."

"Chad," she said, shaking her head and reaching for the phone. "You don't have to do that. I'll just reschedule or something."

He stepped back as he talked to the tow truck company. When he disconnected, he said, "They're on their way. It's no big deal to run you out to Eureka. Levi and I can get dinner and then drive you back."

"I already told her she shouldn't go alone anyway," Levi said, stepping up beside Chad.

For the love of... jeez. Now they were just ganging up on her. Luna opened her mouth to protest, but Chad spoke first.

"Why's that?" Chad asked Levi.

"Too much emotion. I can sense it like a premonition." Levi stared at Luna intently, wringing his hands. "It's charged enough that it makes me nervous."

"That settles it." Chad pressed his hand to the small of Luna's back and nudged her toward his truck a few spaces down. "You don't want to worry Levi, do you?"

Luna rolled her eyes at him but tamped down the urge to smile at them both. It just felt good to have people in her corner worrying about her. While she tended to get frustrated when other people tried to take control of her life, in this case she just felt a ball of warmth in her chest. It was *nice* to be cared for.

The tow truck appeared, and Chad gently took her car key from her hand and ran it over to the driver. After a brief conversation, he jogged back. "Okay. All set. The shop will give you a call in the morning with the diagnosis."

"Okay. Thanks." She glanced at the tow truck driver, waved her appreciation, and then turned to Chad's truck. "Let's go. I don't want this to last all night. In and out. Just long enough for coffee and a piece of pie."

"Pie?" Levi chimed in, his tone nervous.

"Oh, damn," Luna said, pushing her thick hair out of her eyes. "We're meeting at Pies, Pies, and More Pies, but you two can go somewhere else and come back for me if you want."

"No," Levi said thickly. "It's fine." He climbed into the back seat of the truck and closed his eyes as he rested his head against the window.

"You sure?" Chad asked from his spot in the driver's seat. "Does your uncle hang around there? Is there reason to believe we might run into him?"

"No. He was only there to try to force me back to work for him. He holes up in his tiny house until later at night, then he ventures out." Levi let out a humorless laugh. "It's like he's a vampire or something."

"Most drug runners are," Luna said, her voice solemn as if she had reason to know. And she did, too. But now wasn't the time to talk about her experience.

"If you're worried, we can drop you at Luna's," Chad added. "We can bring you back some dinner or something."

Levi shook his head, a determined expression flashing over his features. "Nope. Let's go get some pie."

Luna glanced back at him, admiring his spirit. He was

strong. That was good. He was also a fighter, just like Luna. She had an overwhelming sense that no matter what happened next, Levi was going to make it through this for the better. The feeling settled her, and as she leaned back into the seat, a small bit of the tension she'd been carrying around since she'd received her mother's note drained from her limbs. If Levi could find it within himself to be strong, then so could she.

As Chad pulled out onto the two-lane highway, he reached for Luna's hand, holding it gently while he stroked her palm with his thumb. No words were necessary. He was telling her everything she needed to hear. He was there for her, and that was all that mattered.

CHAPTER 19

*L*una hesitated just before she walked through the door of the restaurant. Her heart sped up, and suddenly it was hard to breathe. Did she want to do this? Was she ready? Her fight or flight reflexes were kicking in, and everything inside of her was screaming for her to run. She knew she didn't owe this woman anything, but she also knew that if she walked away now, she'd always wonder.

And she had questions. So many questions.

"We can walk back to the truck and just drive away if you want," Chad whispered in her ear. His voice washed over her, calming her with his steady support. "Whatever you need."

She glanced over her shoulder and gave him a grateful smile. "Thanks, but I think I need to see this through."

"I figured you would. Just wanted you to know I have your back." He pressed his lips to her temple and gave her a soft kiss. His gentleness made her feel warm and safe even though she knew she was about to walk into something that would likely send her reeling.

"I know. Keep that offer on standby just in case I need to bail? she asked.

His blue eyes turned serious as he nodded. "You got it."

Levi hung back, scanning the parking lot and then peering through the window to get a look at the restaurant. "She's already in there." He jerked his head toward a booth in the back.

Luna followed his gaze and spotted a thin woman with honey-blond hair that hung limply around her gaunt face. She had features that indicated that she'd been pretty once, but now she looked haggard, as if she'd lived a hard life.

It's now or never, Luna told herself. She pushed the door open and strode into the restaurant.

"Good luck," Chad said quietly as he and Levi followed her in.

"Thanks," she said without looking back. Steeling herself, she held her head high and made her way to the table. "Gia?"

The woman's head snapped up, and tears suddenly filled her eyes. "Hope? I mean, Luna? Is that you?"

"Yes," she said stiffly. There was so much emotion rolling off the woman that Luna had no trouble understanding why Levi had been worried about how it would affect her.

Gia stood and slid out of the booth, holding her arms open wide. She reached for Luna and gasped out, "My baby!"

Luna quickly stepped back out of the woman's embrace and placed her hand in front of her in the universal stop motion. "Sorry. I don't know you."

Gia immediately dropped her arms and took her spot in the booth again. Staring down at the plain white coffee mug, she muttered, "Sorry. This isn't a situation one can be prepared for."

She could say that again. Luna let out a quiet sigh and slid into the booth opposite her. The woman's face was heavily lined with wrinkles around her eyes and mouth, making her appear older than Luna originally guessed. But she knew enough about potions to know that they'd likely aged her faster.

"I'm sure you have a lot of questions," Gia said.

"A few," Luna admitted. But instead of asking her mother anything, Luna just sat there looking at her. She thought she'd feel more… well, just more. Instead she just felt numb.

"Okay." Gia's expression was hopeful. "I'll answer anything I can."

"Why?" Luna blurted.

Gia's face flushed, and she twisted her napkin nervously. "Um, why did I give you up?"

"Yeah. Why?" Anger started to curl in Luna's belly, and she wasn't sure exactly why. She'd long ago accepted that she'd been given up for adoption and assumed her birth mom had good reasons. And by the looks of her, Luna had been right. A potions addict had no business raising a child.

"I wasn't in a place where I could take care of you," she said very quietly, not looking at Luna.

"I guess that's pretty obvious." There was bitterness in Luna's tone.

Gia sucked in a breath that turned into a sob.

Luna just sat there waiting as resentment settled in her bones. Listening to the woman break down about a choice she made over twenty years ago frustrated her. Luna was the one who'd been abandoned; she was the one who should be upset. Instead she just felt guilty for not feeling more.

"I need to apologize," Gia said with a sniff. "It's part of my program."

"Right. You're an addict?"

Gia nodded. "Potions. I'm an earth witch and I… well, I had a talent for them."

"And you're clean now?" Luna asked, studying her again. She didn't look like she was high, and her coloring was good, but there was no denying she'd done some hard living over the years.

"I'm clean now," she said, beaming. "The program is working."

"That's good," Luna said softly. She still didn't feel anything, and she started to question Levi's spirit ability. He'd been insistent that the meeting would be too emotional for her, but so far, he was dead wrong.

"I'd like to… um, see you again after this. Maybe start a relationship?" Gia asked hopefully.

Luna stiffened. "I don't know how to answer that."

"It's okay, baby," Gia said, reaching out to cover Luna's hand with her own. "We can take it slow."

A shadow fell over the table, and Luna glanced up expecting to see a waitress had finally come to see if she wanted anything, but instead she looked up into the angry face of Faith Townsend. "Faith, what—"

"What's going on here?" Faith spat out, her eyes glancing back and forth between Gia and Luna. "Do you two know each other?"

"Faith I—" Gia started and then just stared helplessly at Luna.

Luna cleared her throat, having no idea why Faith was so upset. But her boss obviously wasn't pleased she was sitting with this woman. Maybe she'd had trouble with Gia in the past? Luna had no idea what the issue was, but there was no reason to lie. Luna hadn't wanted the town to know about her past in juvy, but this? She had nothing to hide. "Faith, Gia is my biological mother, and—"

"What?" Faith cried, her expression stormy now as her gaze swiveled between them. Then her gaze landed on Luna and something like recognition lit her eyes. She ran a shaky hand through her blond hair and whispered, "Son of a witch. You even look like her a little." She took a step back, shaking her head. "I can't believe this."

She turned her attention to Gia and the anger was back in full force. "You're a real piece of work, you know that? Don't call me again."

Faith spun on her heel and started to stride away, her entire body shaking.

"Faith, wait!" Luna called, sliding out of the booth and running after her.

Faith stopped in her tracks, spinning around so quickly she nearly knocked Luna over. "How dare you come to my spa and lie to me. I can't believe you. Don't come back. You're fired."

"Fired? What?" Luna stared at her, stunned. "But—"

Faith turned and ran to the front door where her fiancé Hunter was waiting for her, his jaw set with tension. She grabbed his hand and the two of them disappeared outside.

Luna's entire body started to tremble.

"Hey," Chad said from right behind her. "Are you all right?"

She turned and glanced up into his handsome face, her mouth working to get words out, but she had no idea what to say. She didn't even know what had just happened.

"Hey," he said, cupping her face with his hands. "What was that with Faith?"

Luna blinked. "She just fired me."

He jerked back, shocked. "Why?"

"I have no idea." Luna glanced past him at Gia, who was still sitting in the booth. Her arms were resting on the table, and her head was down. The slight shake of her shoulders indicated she was crying. "Excuse me," she said to Chad. "I'll be right back."

She brushed past him and slid back into the booth. Her voice was laced with ice as she said, "Start talking. How do you know Faith, and why is she so pissed off?"

Gia lifted her head. Her eyes were watery, but the tears weren't flowing. She sniffed. And when she spoke again, her voice cracked. "Faith is your sister. My legal name is Gabrielle Townsend."

Luna's entire body went ice cold. "Sister?"

Gia… Gabrielle nodded.

"So that means Abby, Yvette, Noel—"

"Your sisters," Gabrielle confirmed.

Luna let out a loud gasp. "And Lincoln? Is he my father?"

"I… um." Gabrielle grimaced. "I don't think so."

"You don't think so?" Luna yelled, her voice going high-pitched. "Does that mean you don't actually know?"

She shook her head. "I was involved with someone before I left Lincoln. That other man, he could be your father."

"What's his name," Luna demanded.

She shook her head again. "I just knew him as Michael."

Luna's stomach turned. "Oh, gods. I'm going to be sick." She bolted out of the booth and ran to the women's restroom. Once she was in one of the small stalls, she stood over the toilet, her mouth watering as her stomach continued to churn. She took deep breaths, over and over again, until the nausea cleared. But that didn't keep her head from spinning.

She had sisters, and maybe had found a father who surely hadn't known she existed. He wouldn't have let Gabrielle give up one of his daughters if he'd known. She was sure of it.

Lincoln Townsend was all about family. Her eyes burned with the thought that she might've grown up as a Townsend in Keating Hollow. It was enough to gut her.

"Luna?" Chad's voice held a note of panic. "I'm coming in."

She wiped at her eyes and stepped out of the stall just in time to see him move through the door.

"Hey," he said, rushing forward and wrapping his arms around her. "I was worried about you."

She pressed her head to his shoulder and just held on.

"I'm sorry, Hope," he said. "You don't deserve any of this."

It didn't escape her notice that he'd used her given name, but even though she'd left that name behind years ago, she liked hearing it on his lips. It was the name he'd called her before, when he was the only person in her life that she trusted.

"Take me home," she whispered. "I just want to get out of here."

"Anything you want." He pressed a kiss to the top of her head and then wrapped her hand in his as he led her back out into the restaurant.

Gabrielle jumped out of the booth as soon as they passed her. "Luna, wait."

Luna shook her head, and with Chad's firm hand on her back, she kept going. Levi held the front door open for her, and without even a glance backward, she escaped into the dark parking lot.

CHAPTER 20

*S*ilence filled the truck cab all the way back to Keating Hollow. Luna had brushed off both Chad's and Levi's attempts to ask if she was okay, and instead of pushing it, they'd both let her be.

Chad could only imagine what was going through her head. She had sisters. And maybe a father. And a life that had been stolen from her when her mother had given her up for adoption. It must've been a brutal blow. But what had made it worse was the altercation between her and Faith, Luna's boss and friend. Chad just hoped that after the shock wore off, the two could talk and repair the damage their mother had wrought.

"Do you want me to stop and get you something to eat?" Chad asked as they turned onto Main Street in Keating Hollow.

She shook her head.

"There's food in the fridge. I can make her something," Levi said from the back seat. His voice was low and full of concern.

"I'm not hungry," Luna said and pressed her head against the window.

Levi didn't respond. Chad watched him in the rearview mirror as he slumped lower in his seat, his eyes cast downward.

Chad clutched the wheel tighter and turned right, then left, and finally pulled into Luna's driveway.

She was out of the truck and running to the door of the cottage before he could even get the vehicle in park. Chad watched her as she stumbled inside and disappeared into the darkness of the house.

"She's vomiting," Levi said with a slight shudder.

"Nerves?" Chad asked.

"Yeah." Levi undid his seatbelt and climbed out of the truck.

Chad met him near the walkway, and the pair followed Luna into the house. Levi went straight to the kitchen while Chad went upstairs to Luna's bedroom. The light was on, but the bathroom door was closed, and the water was running. After a moment, he decided she was in the shower and left to go find Levi again.

The teenager was in the kitchen heating tomato soup and working on a grilled cheese. "I know she said she isn't hungry, but she should try to eat something."

Chad grinned at him. "Good call."

He shrugged. "My mom used to always make grilled cheese and tomato soup any time I was sick or upset. Even if I didn't eat it, the fact that she went through the trouble always made me feel a little better."

Chad clasped his hand over the teenager's shoulder. "It's good to be taken care of every now and then."

Levi gave him a nod and went back to monitoring the grilled cheese.

The pinched expression on Levi's face made Chad wonder when Levi had last been cared for. Certainly, the night he and Luna had picked him up and taken him to the healer, but before that? He feared it was far, far too long.

"Here you go. Take this up to her." Levi handed him a plate with a cup of the soup and the grilled cheese already cut in half.

"You do it," Chad urged. "I'll be up in a minute."

Levi chewed on his bottom lip. "You're sure? I have no idea what to say."

"You don't have to say anything. Your presence will be enough." Chad opened the cabinets and started rummaging around.

"What are you looking for?" Levi asked as he moved toward the stairs.

He reached up and grabbed a container of cocoa. "Just taking stock of the options."

"Dessert?" Levi asked, clearly reading Chad's mind.

Chad chuckled. "Chocolate is always a good idea."

"No argument here. I'll be right down to help you." Levi disappeared up the stairs while Chad gathered a bunch more ingredients, and after texting Barb for her recipe, he got to work on a batch of double chocolate cupcakes.

"LUNA?" Chad called from the hallway just outside her bedroom. The door was cracked open, and a sliver of light spilled out onto the hardwood floor.

"Yeah," she said softly.

He pushed the door open and found her sitting up in her bed. Her hair was up in a messy bun on top of her head, and she was wearing a faded T-shirt and soft pajama pants. A pair of glasses rested on her nose as she stared down at a tablet. "Levi and I made cupcakes."

Her lips twitched into a tiny smile. "That was sweet of you."

He glanced over at the plate Levi had brought up for her over an hour ago. There were a few bites taken from the grilled cheese, but the soup was gone. Good. She'd managed to eat something at least.

"Here." He handed her one of the cupcakes and put the second one on her nightstand next to the plate.

Footsteps sounded behind him, indicating that Levi had followed him upstairs.

The teenager swept into the room. "I'm just grabbing your dinner dishes," he said. "Was it okay?"

Luna nodded at him. "Thank you. It was just what I needed."

Levi frowned and ran a hand over his brow. "You're still really upset."

Chad peered at her. She seemed a lot better than she had an hour earlier. What was Levi seeing that he wasn't?

"I'm just…" She waved a hand. "It's a lot to process."

Levi sat down on the edge of the bed. "I wish I could do something to fix it. My magic means I sense it all, but I can't change anything. It's frustrating! What's the point of being magical if I can't help anyone?"

Luna's eyes lit with interest as she studied him. "Did you know I work for a healer a couple of days a week?"

"I remember you saying something about that," he said.

Luna removed her glasses and tilted her head. "Why don't you come with me next time and meet Healer Snow? She might have some suggestions."

"Sure. I guess." But his frown only deepened as he watched her. "That doesn't help you now though."

Luna's mask suddenly fell, and her seemingly normal expression vanished. Her eyes were wary and her skin pale as she sucked in a deep, shaky breath. "I think I just need to get some sleep. Let my subconscious work through everything." She placed the uneaten cupcake on her nightstand and leaned against the headboard with her eyes closed. "I'm sure tomorrow will be better."

"Right," Levi said, grabbing the dinner plate and rising from the bed. As he passed Chad, he pressed his free hand to his chest and whispered, "Don't leave her alone. It feels to me like her heart is breaking in two."

"I won't," Chad said automatically, pain striking his own heart.

Once Levi disappeared, Chad took his place beside her on the bed. He picked up her hand and cradled it in both of his. "I'm not going to ask how you're doing. I can see for myself."

She let out a humorless laugh. "It's that obvious?"

He lifted her palm and kissed it. "Anyone would be shaken up. Are you worried about your job at the spa?"

Luna nodded. "I know we need to talk, but the uncertainty… it's what's giving me a stomach ache. If I don't have a steady, full-time income, I can't stay here. Levi and I… we'll have to find something cheaper until I can get a new job."

"Well, you've already got one client." He squeezed her hand. "You can put me on the books for three days a week. Whatever it is you're doing to my hand, it's the best it's felt since the accident."

"Really?" She closed her fingers around his damaged hand. It still radiated trauma, but it did feel a little better than it had when she'd first massaged him.

"Really." He pressed a kiss to her cheek. "Thank you."

She started to run her fingers over his, letting her magic slip over his skin. A slight shudder ran through him with her touch, the kind that warmed him from the inside out, more from the connection they'd formed than anything that was inherently sexual. He just felt closer to her when she was caring for him. And right then, he wanted to be the one who cared for her, wanted to show her he could shoulder her burdens with her.

Chad gently pulled his hand from hers, whispering, "That feels wonderful, but let me take care of you now."

"I don't—"

"Shh." He pressed one finger to her lips and tucked a fallen lock of hair behind one ear. "You're exhausted. Let me help you relax so you can get some sleep."

She raked her gaze over him and then lifted one eyebrow in question. "And you're going to do that how?"

He chuckled, knowing what she was asking. She wanted to know if *relax* was code for *sex*. It wasn't. "I'm not a professional or anything, but how about you let me massage you for once? How about it? I could work your neck, shoulders, and back. Ease some of that tension away?"

"Just a massage?" she asked.

"Just a massage," he echoed.

Her guarded expression vanished, and she gave him a slight smile. "That sounds nice."

"Lay on your stomach," he said.

She did as he asked and lifted her arms over her head as he moved to straddle her. Chad pressed his hands against her back, running them over her T-shirt. Her muscles were tight under his touch, and he did his best to knead out the kinks.

After a while she said, "Chad?"

"Yeah?"

"I want your hands on my bare skin."

He stilled, his body already tingling with anticipation. There was no denying he wanted her. He'd wanted her since the moment he'd first spotted her in Keating Hollow a few weeks ago. But he couldn't let anything happen. Not that night. Not after what had happened at the restaurant. Not to mention there was a teenager in the house.

Taking the decision out of his hands, she lifted slightly and tugged the T-shirt off, leaving her torso completely bare. She laid back down on the bed, her head turned to the side with a small smile claiming her lips.

"Hope," he said, his breath catching.

"Luna," she corrected, but her smile only widened.

"Right." Her skin was creamy white and so soft as he once again pressed his hands to her back.

Her eyes fluttered closed. "That's really nice."

He wasn't doing anything but caressing her skin, but faint tingles of electricity were sparking under his fingertips and he never wanted to stop. He held himself over her, his hands running up and down, exploring every inch of her perfect flesh. And when he couldn't stand it anymore, he leaned down and pressed a soft kiss to her neck. "I should go."

"Do you have to?" she asked, looking up at him through sleepy eyes.

"No. But we both know I should."

"I guess that's true." She reached for her T-shirt and a moment later, she'd wiggled up to her knees, her back still to him as she pulled the garment back on. But instead of telling him goodnight, she curled up on her side and pulled him down next to her. She looked up at him. "Thank you. That was wonderful."

"I'm sure my technique could use a lot of work, but I tried."

She threaded her hand into his hair, pulled his head down, and without hesitation she pressed a soft kiss to his lips. "You could have a career in massage therapy. You're a natural." Her eyes glinted. "You were right. This was exactly what I needed." Luna let out a contented sigh. Then she rolled over so that Chad was spooning her from behind and tugged on his hand so that his arm was wrapped around her.

Gods, she felt good against the length of his body. He was acutely aware that he'd be happy to stay right there for forever or as long as she let him.

Luna snuggled in closer and then on a whisper, she said, "Goodnight, Chad."

He pressed another kiss just below her ear, inhaled her clean soap scent, and said, "Night, sweet girl."

CHAPTER 21

*L*una woke the next morning draped over Chad's chest. His breathing was deep and even, indicating that he was still sleeping. She lay there, unmoving, just enjoying the feel of him under her. For years she'd long to wake up just like this. Only she hadn't imagined that they'd be fully clothed. Her lips curved into a smile and she almost laughed. She was almost twenty-one years old, and because she was lying with Chad, she felt seventeen again. At least she did when it came to all the feelings swarming in her chest.

The urge to press her lips to his neck and slowly wake him up was right there at the surface. All she had to do was tilt her head and she'd have access to his warm skin. But as she glanced at the clock, reality crashed in around her.

Last night's news had sent her mind reeling. She'd found a mother who appeared to be unstable at best and an entire family she'd never known about. A family she already admired and would've done just about anything to have while growing up.

She'd already decided to go into the spa and talk to Faith.

Her boss—sister—had been in shock. Luna had too for that matter. Surely they could work something out. It was obvious to Luna that Faith thought she'd been betrayed. Luna just needed to convince her sister that she had been in the dark just as much as everyone else had.

Careful to not wake Chad, Luna rolled out of bed and disappeared into her bathroom. Twenty minutes later, she emerged wearing her uniform of black yoga pants and a white T-shirt. She'd pulled her blond hair back into a braid that fell down her back and applied just enough makeup to cover her pale skin and hide her tired eyes. She'd slept last night, but the emotional turmoil had left her exhausted.

She'd just gotten to the door when she heard Chad say, "Hey."

Luna turned and smiled at the sleepy man in her bed. "Good morning."

He blinked and pushed himself up. His brows furrowed as he took her in. "You're going to work?"

"Yep. Faith was upset. I'm going to talk to her before I let her fire me for something I had no control over."

"Good." He smiled at her, and his sleepy voice was gravelly as he added, "But come here first."

She was powerless to stop herself, and she quickly made her way to the side of the bed, sitting next to him.

He pressed his hand to her cheek and leaned in giving her a soft kiss on the lips. "Last night was perfect."

She chuckled. "Which part? Meeting my mother or me drooling on your chest while I slept?"

"The drooling part," he said without hesitation. "Are we still on for dinner tomorrow night?"

"Yes," she said, staring at his red lips.

"Good." His gaze roamed all over her, and his hand

tightened on her thigh where it had been resting lightly. "Levi and I are going to start working on my shop today. If you get a break, come on by and we'll go to lunch."

"If I even still have a job," she said quietly.

"You will."

Silence fell as they continued to stare at each other.

"I should go," Luna said.

"Right." Chad wrapped his arm around her waist and pulled her into him, giving her another soft kiss. "Good luck."

Her lips tingled with the light kisses, and it was all she could do to not climb into bed with him and forget about going to talk to Faith. The woman had fired her. Being late wouldn't be an issue would it?

"Go," he urged, but it was obvious by his hold on her he didn't mean it.

Still, the word propelled her into action. "Time to save my job. See you later." Luna strode toward the door and glanced back just once to take in the site of Chad lounging in her bed. Yeah, she could definitely get used to that.

Nerves jumped in Luna's belly as she waited for Faith to appear at the spa. She was sitting in the front reception area in one of the chairs, drumming her fingernails on the side table.

"Are you going to tell me what's up?" Lena asked from behind the desk. The woman's dark eyes were narrowed as she studied Luna. "There aren't any early appointments on the books. Who are you waiting for?"

"Faith," she said. "I need to talk to her before we start the day."

Lena gave her a strange look. "Why don't you just go into her office?"

"This is fine."

"If you say so." Lena kept casting her questioning glances for the next half hour until the bell on the door chimed and Faith walked in.

"Luna doesn't work here anymore," Faith said to Lena. "We need to rebook all of her appointments."

"What?" Lena frowned. "But she's—"

"She misled me," Faith said. "It's done. If you need me to stay late or come in early for rebookings, I'll do it. Just let me know."

Luna, well aware that Faith hadn't noticed her when she'd strode in, stood and cleared her throat.

Startled, Faith jerked her head toward Luna and then scowled. "You shouldn't be here."

"We need to talk." Luna wasn't going anywhere until she'd had her say.

"That's not necessary." Faith straightened her spine and started to move in the direction of her office.

"I just found out last night that Gia's my mother," Luna blurted. "Or rather, I just met her for the first time last night. Prior to that I had no idea who she was or that you're—"

"Fine," she barked, cutting Luna off probably so that she couldn't reveal any personal details in front of Lena. "We can talk in my office. But I only have ten minutes before my first appointment."

"Um, should I still cancel Luna's appointments?" Lena asked.

"Yes," Faith said at the same time Luna said, "No."

The two women stared at each other.

Luna let out a sigh. "Don't cancel them. I'll honor my

appointments today. And after we talk, if you still want me to go, then I will. But give me a chance first, please."

Uncertainty flittered over Faith's face, and Luna knew then that this situation could be salvaged. She just needed to get past Faith's defenses. "Fine." Faith glanced at Lena. "Luna will work today, but don't take any new appointments for her until further notice."

"Got it." Lena waited until Faith turned to walk toward her office again before she grimaced in sympathy at Luna and mouthed, *What's going on?*

Luna shook her head and followed her sister down the hallway.

The minute Faith's door was closed, she rounded on Luna. "Are you really trying to tell me that you ended up in Keating Hollow, working at *my spa* and you didn't know that we're sisters?"

"Yes," Luna said, evenly. "That's exactly what I'm saying."

"That's crap. Come on, Luna. Coincidences like that don't just happen. Why are you lying to me?" Faith's willowy frame vibrated with anger. "Just be honest with me."

Luna tilted her head at her sister, and then with practiced calm, she reached into her pocket and pulled out the card Gia had sent to the spa. She held it out to Faith. "Do you remember the letter I got last week that didn't have a return address?"

"Yeah."

Luna shoved the note into Faith's hand. "This was it. Read it."

Faith took the card and glanced at it. Whatever she saw made her do a double take, because she lifted the card and scanned it, one hand covering her mouth.

"That was the first time I heard from her. Prior to that, the only thing I knew about my birth mom was that she was from the Eureka area," Luna said.

"Did you come here looking for her?" Faith asked as she sank down onto her overstuffed couch.

Luna, still standing in the middle of the room, shook her head. "I actually came to Eureka because of my job there with Healer Snow. I got the job here because I'm a trained massage therapist and you were hiring. I didn't know anything, Faith. I didn't come here under false pretenses. I swear."

Faith sat back in her couch and let out a long breath. She closed her eyes as if she were pained. Finally, she asked, "If that's true, how did Gabby know to look for you, here?"

Luna shrugged. "I did submit paperwork with the adoption center that said I was open to meeting my biological parents. I kept it updated with how to contact me. It wouldn't have been that hard for her to find me."

Faith stared at her hands, her body completely still. "I'm sorry I tried to fire you."

Relief rushed through Luna's veins as she processed the words. *Tried to fire you.* That meant she hadn't lost her job. Thank the gods. "Thanks for that. I really can't afford to be unemployed."

Faith nodded. "I can imagine." She raised her eyes and met Luna's gaze. "But I'm not ready to..." She waved a hand between them. "I need time to process this. I'm sure you have questions about our family, but I—"

"It's okay," Luna said, letting her off the hook. "We both need to get to work anyway. We can deal with the fact that we're related later. Did you tell your sisters?"

Faith nodded. "They're your sisters too, you know."

How had Luna managed to gain four sisters overnight? And were they all freaking out as much as Faith was? If so, she wasn't sure she was eager to spend time with any of them. The one she did want to talk to was Lincoln Townsend. But that would need to wait. "I know," she said simply. "But I'm sure they need time to adjust, too."

Faith barked out a laugh. "That's true for me and Noel. But watch out for Abby and Yvette. They tend to take things head on. And my dad is already asking about meeting you." She reached into her pocket and pulled out a business card. After scribbling a number on the back, she passed it to Luna. "Call him when you're ready."

Luna stared at the card, both grateful and terrified. She desperately wanted Lincoln Townsend to be her father. She couldn't imagine him rejecting her. But if he wasn't, then who exactly was? Some potions addict? Her heart turned to ice at the thought.

A knock sounded on the door. "Faith?" Lena said. "Your appointment is here."

"Right." She jumped up off the couch and went for the door. Just before she opened it, she glanced over her shoulder and said, "I'll tell her to resume your appointments."

Luna just nodded. She'd moved on from worrying about her job to stressing big time about Lincoln Townsend.

But a few minutes later when Lena popped in again, it was time to work. Luna put the card in her back pocket and pushed her tangled family mess to the side so she could concentrate on her clients. It didn't exactly work. By lunch, she'd imagined a dozen different scenarios where she was welcomed into the Townsend family and twice as many more where they all rejected her. Somewhere deep down, she knew her fears were irrational. The Townsends were good people. But Luna had never had family that loved her. That constant disappointment did something to a person. And it wasn't anything good.

CHAPTER 22

Trees lined the long driveway up to the Townsend home that sat on the edge of town. The Townsend property sprawled along the base of the foothills and looked like something out of a fairy tale. Bright flowers in almost every color were in bloom, the natural fields were green, and when Luna rounded the final curve in the road, the sun illuminated the large cabin-style home.

It was gorgeous. What would it have been like to grow up there? Would she have appreciated it if she had? She shook her head. What good was there in asking that question? Her first memory of a home was a small two-bedroom house with her adoptive mom. It had just been the two of them after her adoptive dad took off on them when Luna was only two. Luna remembered it as a happy time. Her mother was a sweet woman who spent most of her time in her gardens or reading to Luna. She couldn't remember anything about their life being fancy, but it was the only place where she'd had her own room up until she'd been released from juvy on her eighteenth birthday.

After her adoptive mom died when Luna was only five, she'd slept on couches, in rooms with three bunk beds, and in apartments that barely had enough room for two people, let alone five. At the last house, with her foster mom Pam, she'd had three foster brothers and one foster sister. That meant Luna had one roommate while the boys had three. And they'd all hated it there. Pam didn't give a crap about anything other than her potion business and her shady boyfriend Leo. The kids were just a paycheck to Pam, or maybe a cover for her illegal drug business. Frankly, Luna didn't care. All she'd wanted was to get out.

But this life? The one in Keating Hollow? It was what she'd always dreamed of as a kid. Would the family she always wanted welcome her, or would she always be the outsider who Gabrielle Townsend had thrown away?

There was only one way to find out. Luna stopped in front of the pretty house, put her car in park, and took a deep breath. She could do this. More importantly, she *wanted* to do this, no matter how nerve wracking it turned out to be. With slightly shaking hands, Luna pulled the key out of the ignition and climbed out of the car. The next thing she knew, she was on the porch, knocking on the door.

The door swung open and the man who she prayed was her father smiled at her. "You made it." Lincoln Townsend opened the door wider for her. "Come on in. I'll get us something to drink."

Luna followed Lin and studied the older man. He was tall with neatly trimmed gray hair, and he had steel-colored eyes. He'd gained a little weight since the last time she'd seen him, which was a good sign he was feeling better. She'd heard he'd been battling cancer but that he'd recently gone into remission.

They stepped into a large living room area, and Luna

paused to take in the room. The overstuffed couch was slightly worn, but still inviting. There was a large metal pentacle over the fireplace, the only indication that witches lived there. And toward the back of the room was an open concept kitchen. Lin was milling around, pulling down ingredients to make something, though she wasn't sure what. And she found she didn't care, not once she got a glimpse of the back of the property through the wide glass French doors. The large clearing was lovely with a stone outdoor patio complete with a built-in fire pit. It looked like the perfect place for a family gathering. One she was dying to be included in.

"Here," Lin said gently, pressing a warm mug into her hands. "Do you want to take a tour of the property while we talk?"

"Yes," Luna said, relief rushing through her. It was always easier to get through the hard stuff when there was something else to focus on.

"This way."

Still clutching her mug, Luna followed Lin down a hallway and into the garage. He waved a hand at a four-person golf cart. "Want to drive?" he asked.

Luna laughed. "Maybe later? I'd really like to just see your gorgeous property."

"You got it." He climbed into the driver's seat, waited for her to get situated next to him, and then backed out of the garage and maneuvered the cart around to the back of the house toward the family's apple orchard. He was staring straight ahead when he said, "I bet you have a ton of questions."

"I… um, yes, but there's really just one I need to know." Her face was hot, and she was sure her cheeks had turned bright red.

"I think we're both anxious to know the answer to that

question." He turned down a path that led through the orchard. "How old are you, Luna?"

Luna swallowed hard. "I'll be twenty-one in a few months."

Lincoln turned to her, his eyes full of hope and regret and something else she couldn't quite pinpoint. "It's possible then."

The words shot straight to her heart, sending ripples of both joy and pure pain through her. She wanted this. She wanted this man to be her father. It didn't matter that she barely knew him. She knew enough to know that he'd never shut her out. Luna's voice was shaky as she said, "I don't want to get my hopes up."

Lin stayed silent, and Luna was afraid to look at him. But then he reached over and took her hand in his and said, "Whatever the outcome, you're family now. Whether you use the name or keep the one you grew up with, you're a Townsend now. You have four sisters and a man who wishes with all of his heart that he'd known about you and been there for you while you were growing up."

Hot tears fell down Luna's cheeks. His words were too good to be true. No one had ever accepted her so unconditionally before.

Well, no one but Chad.

"Thank you," Luna said, patting at her cheeks. "But you don't have to say that. Gia, err Gabrielle, says she's pretty sure that you're not my... Well, it's the reason she gave me up in the first place."

Lin's hand tightened around Luna's. "Sweet girl, if Gabby hadn't run off, even if she'd told me you weren't mine, I'd have raised you as if you were. There's no question about that."

Luna turned to stare at him, her mouth moving but not working. Finally, she forced out, "But why?"

He let out a humorless chuckle, but when he met her gaze

LOVE OF THE WITCH

there was nothing there but sincerity. "I loved her. She was the mother of my children, and before she got hooked on potions, she was a wonderful partner. If she'd come to me for help, I'd have moved heaven and earth to help her get clean. In the end, she made her choices. And that's something we've all had to live with. I believe you ended up with the worst of it."

There was no denying that. If Luna's adoptive mom hadn't passed away at such a young age, Luna might've felt differently. It was hard to say. But she'd loved her mom and had fond memories of her early childhood. It was after her mom's death that things got bad. But all Luna said was, "I have a good life now."

"You have no idea how happy that makes me," Lin said with a smile. "Now, we'll have the DNA test because it seems like the right thing to do. Secrets never solve anything, but to be honest, it doesn't matter what that test says. You're a Townsend. You're one of us, and if you'll let me, I'd like to be your dad."

His words had completely knocked her off her axis. Why was Lincoln Townsend being so kind to her? And why was he so ready to accept her as his before the DNA test? They'd met before, a few times at the brewery and at a couple of town social events, but they didn't really know one another. Or at least not enough for this man to embrace her so quickly and without question.

"Luna?" he prompted.

"Yeah?"

"Would that be okay with you?" The kind, hopeful expression in his gaze made the tears fall again. She managed a nod but couldn't get any words out.

Lin stopped the cart, jumped out, and jogged around to her side. After tugging her off the seat, he wrapped his arms around her. "I'm so sorry, Luna. You have no idea how sorry I am."

He was talking as if he knew her past, and she wondered who'd told him. There was only one person who could've. Betrayal made her head swim, and as the anger took over, her tears dried. She pulled back, carefully extracting herself from Lin's embrace. "What did Chad tell you?"

"Chad?" he asked, looking confused. "Barb's stepson?"

"Yeah. That Chad. What did he tell you about me?" Her entire body had heated, and all the stress of learning about her biological parents rushed to the surface. "He had no right to tell you or anyone what my life was like before I came to Keating Hollow."

"Luna," he said softly. "I didn't talk to Chad. I talked to Faith."

"She's not very happy about this new development," Luna said.

Lin sucked in a deep breath. "She's not happy with her mother. Faith needs time to process. I know my girl, and she'll come around. And once she does, she'll be all in. You'll see."

Luna nodded and was surprised by how much she wanted that. After Faith's initial reaction, she'd resigned herself to the fact that her sisters might never fully accept her. It was something she was prepared for. Actually, it was the only thing she was prepared for. Letting herself dream of being one big happy family was just too risky. Her heart couldn't take the rejection if she let herself long for the one thing she'd always wanted—family—only to have it crash and burn.

But Faith had talked to Lincoln straight away about her. She must not have told him anything too disparaging if he wanted a relationship with her. Luna filed through her brain, considering everything she'd ever said to the woman. She'd been careful to keep the details of her past vague, not talking about foster care, or her adoptive mom's early death, or even how she managed after she turned eighteen. Those were all painful memories for her, and not something she wanted to talk about.

"She told me you said you didn't have any family and that you hoped that Keating Hollow would be a place where you could put down roots because that's something you'd never had before."

Okay, she had said that. But so what? That wasn't tragic. Just a fact of life. "You don't need to be sorry for that," she said softly.

Lin shoved his hands in his pockets and stared out at his orchard. "Maybe not, but I do anyway. If things with Gabby hadn't gone so far south, maybe all of this could've been different. Maybe if I'd been more open to her issues, or noticed sooner, or insisted on help…" He frowned and hung his head almost as if in defeat. "Mostly I'm just sorry you didn't have a chance to grow up here with your sisters." He lifted his head and met Luna's gaze. "I would've liked that very much."

Luna didn't know what to say or even how to feel. So instead she said, "Tell me about your orchard."

Lin cast her a smile, walked back around the cart, and climbed in. After she did the same, he said, "Let me show you the first section we planted."

CHAPTER 23

*C*had pulled the truck into the space in front of Incantation Café and put the vehicle in park. He twisted to glance back at Levi. The kid was dressed in ripped jeans, a vintage Stones T-shirt, and had put some product in his hair that made his curls appear perpetually wet. And was that eyeliner? Chad smiled to himself. The teenager had a hint of a smile on his face, and for the first time since they'd met, he appeared happy.

"Take this." Luna held out some cash to him.

Levi shook his head. "No, Luna. I can't."

"Yes. You can." She reached back and stuffed it into his hand. "Think of it as allowance or something."

Levi stared down at the bills. "But I haven't done anything to deserve an allowance."

Luna shrugged. "You've made dinner and cleaned the kitchen ever since you moved in. If it makes you feel better, you can be in charge of the landscaping. Mowing, weeding, raking, etc. Deal?"

"You better take her up on it, Levi," Chad said. "Otherwise

we'll be here all night, and you'll be responsible for messing up my date." He winked at the kid. "Do me a favor and get out, would ya?"

Levi rolled his eyes but stuffed the money in his pocket and pushed the door open. "Thanks, Luna," he said softly.

"You're welcome," she said. "Have a good time tonight. Call if you need anything. Anything at all. Or if you need a ride home. Okay?"

"I'll be fine," Levi said.

"Of course you will." Luna nodded. "Even so, we're only one phone call away if anything goes south. Understand?"

He chuckled, and his eyes started to sparkle with amusement. "I understand. And I will if I need anything. Now go. Enjoy your night in Eureka. And don't miss curfew. I'm told it's eleven pm."

"Eleven-thirty," Luna said.

Levi laughed. "Don't want to cut the night short?"

Luna's face turned a pretty shade of pink.

Chad grinned, enjoying their banter and Luna's mild embarrassment. "Go on," Chad said. "Go do teenager stuff. We've got someplace to be."

"Don't let me hold you up," Levi said, taking a step out of the truck and up onto the cobblestone sidewalk.

Chad put the truck in reverse while Luna waved.

And just as they were pulling away, Levi shouted, "Don't forget the condoms!"

Luna gaped at the teenager.

Chad just laughed.

"Can you believe he just said that?" she asked.

Chad raised one eyebrow at her. "The bigger question is why are you so shocked? He's a teenager who has seen a lot of crap, not some sheltered kid."

Luna leaned back against the seat and closed her eyes. "Guh. I know you're right. The things I said to people when I was his age…" Her voice trailed off and she looked at Chad, her eyes narrowed. "Is it weird that you knew me when I was his age?"

"Nope," he said. "Not at all." Chad turned onto the two-lane highway that led to Eureka. "The truth is I never saw you as anything other than a kid who needed help getting on her feet back then. This?" He waved a hand between them. "What's going on now is completely new for me. And you, Luna Scott, are anything but a kid now."

That flush on her cheeks turned brighter. "I, um… I used to have a crush on you."

Something swelled in Chad's chest. He'd figured as much but had never wanted to acknowledge the possibility for a couple of reasons. First, he hadn't felt the same back then. And second, he'd known if they were going to go ahead with the plan of her living in his house once she turned eighteen, they needed clear boundaries.

"You knew, didn't you?" she accused.

Chad nodded. "I guessed. But even though I cared a great deal about what would happen to you once you aged out of the system, that was never the reason why. I wasn't looking to date you. I just wanted to give you a chance to make it in the world once you were on your own."

"And what about now, Chad?" she asked, her voice so low and smoky it was like a caress on his senses.

"Now?" He chuckled. "You already know the answer to that. There's no point in denying the chemistry that keeps pulling us together." He reached across the truck and pulled her hand into his.

Luna ran her thumb over the back of his palm, sending tingles over his skin that made him let out a tiny groan.

"That feels really good," he said.

She glanced up at him, frowning as she started to probe his hand with her fingers. "Your tendons are tight again. Does your hand always cramp up this fast? It's only been a few days since the last massage."

"No. I might have overdone it at the music store today." He squeezed her hand to indicate it wasn't that bad and had to bite back a wince. Son of a… what had he done to himself? "It's all right," he said.

"Are you ever going to tell me how this happened?" she asked. "What really happened, I mean?"

Oh, hell. He'd meant to come clean with her about that night three months ago. The night that had ruined his career and sent him spiraling down a completely different path. He just didn't want to do it right before their first date. But maybe he knew he had to. If he put her off, she was likely to feel betrayed. "I actually meant to tell you sooner," he started. "But we got interrupted and…" He shrugged. "It's been a little hectic.

"You're not wrong about that." Luna's powerful touch skated over his skin, her magic slowly but surely easing the tension in his palm. "But we're here now, and I'm listening."

"Okay." He steeled himself. That night he'd told her about his call to the cops that ultimately ended up with her in jail is the night he should've told her about the rest. But then Levi had called, and his priorities had shifted instantly. "You know how you said that Pam told you she'd give you your school money back after you delivered the potions to the dealer?"

"Yeah. But what does that have to do with your hand?"

"She never had any intention of giving you that money back," Chad said. "She spent it on—"

"She gave it back to me when I was released from juvy," Luna said. "A messenger met me outside of the gates with a box and all of it was there. In fact, there was even a couple hundred extra. I always figured she felt guilty for what happened to me and that it was her way of making it up to me." Luna's tone was bitter as she spit the words out. "Like two hundred dollars could give me back months of my life. Pathetic."

"Luna," Chad said, pulling his hand from hers while he made the turn into Eureka. "Pam didn't send that money or set up the short-term rental. I did." He couldn't see her face; he was too focused on the road. But he did hear her startled gasp. Then there was silence. Chad glanced over at her. She was staring at him with wide eyes. "Hey," he said softly. "Say something."

"I—what the hell, Chad?" she yelled. "Seriously? You just coughed up a few thousand dollars and didn't even tell me? I spent all this time thinking Pam had at least a sliver of a soul, but it turns out I was right the first time. My foster mother only cared about herself, and you decided to play savior but kept that from me. Why? Why didn't you tell me right away? Why didn't you leave me a note along with the rental agreement? And for god's sake, what does any of this have to do with your hand?"

He winced. He'd known he should've told her sooner, but he hadn't expected her to be that angry. "I was the one who was responsible for landing you in jail," he said. "It had only been a few months, but my level of guilt was… well, it was off the charts. I didn't leave a note because I didn't think I deserved any credit. Don't you see, Hope? I blamed myself for a long, long time. I sent the money because I just wanted you to have a chance."

"You sent it because you felt guilty," she snapped. "Well, congratulations. I absolve you. Your conscience is clear."

The fire in her gaze told him there wasn't anything he could say in that moment to make things right between them. She was too angry and needed time to process. But he couldn't just drop it. There was more she needed to know. "My conscience isn't clear. I doubt it ever will be."

She let out an irritated huff. "I'm not, nor have I ever been, your problem to fix, Chad."

"I know." He did, too. Still, he'd never stop trying to protect her. He just cared too much. And he hated that he'd ever been a part of anything that had hurt her. "Leo had plans to bring you back to Pam's after you were released from jail."

Luna blinked at him. Then she sucked in a breath and said, "What?"

Chad pulled into the parking lot of the large Victorian where the evening's event was being held. After killing the engine, he turned to look at her. "After you were arrested, I went to your house to find out what happened. Leo was on a bender, talking about how when you got out, you'd have no choice but to work for him. We got into it. A few punches were thrown, and the cops were called. He took off before they arrived."

"Like I was ever going to go back to that house," Luna scoffed.

"I knew as long as you had resources, you'd never do that," Chad said with a nod. "So I called Pam about a week before your release. I tried to talk her into giving you the money she stole from you, but of course it was long gone. She said something about you making it back in no time once you came crawling back to them. Leo was already planning on keeping an eye on you. Pam said she knew you wouldn't want to, but when times got tough enough, Leo would lure you back."

Luna pressed a hand to her stomach and shook her head. "Never."

Chad desperately wanted to reach out and touch her, but he kept his hands to himself. Now wasn't the time. "If the company I went to work for hadn't been on tour, I would've been there to meet you myself when you were released. But since I was in Europe at the time, I hired someone to hand deliver you the money. It was the only thing I could think of to make sure you had what you needed so that Leo wouldn't manipulate you into his drug business... or worse."

Her eyes narrowed as she studied him. Her utter defiance was palpable as she asked, "Do you really think I would've let him get his claws into me?"

"No. Not if you could help it," Chad said gently. "But you were eighteen, fresh out of jail and had no family to rely on, so I did the only thing I could to try to help."

"All without leaving a note. Or even a phone number. Hell, Chad. What if your money hadn't worked? What if Leo had gotten to me anyway? What would you have done then?"

He felt his cheeks heat, and he glanced away as she added, "You remember the woman who was there with the money?"

"Yes," she practically barked out.

"She also kept an eye on you. She was a private investigator. I asked her to check in on you periodically just to make sure you were safe."

More silence filled the vehicle.

Chad stared straight ahead, knowing he'd crossed lines. He should've told her. Should've given her his phone number and asked her to keep in touch. Let her know he was behind the cash. But he'd been so guilty and so unavailable while they toured Europe. If she had gotten into trouble, it wasn't as if he could just hop in a car and go kick Leo's ass.

"You had someone spy on me." Her voice was ice cold.

"Not spy. More like watch over," he said.

"Call it whatever you want, but you could've told me. You should've told me."

"You're right. I should've."

Luna blew out a frustrated breath. "This isn't how I expected the evening to go."

"I know." Chad closed his eyes. "I'd take you home, but I have to play a few songs after dinner. If you want, you can take my truck. I'll figure something out, some way to get back to Keating Hollow."

She let out a heavy sigh. "No, Chad. I'm not taking your truck. I'm frustrated and upset, but I'm not going to abandon you here. Let's just go in."

"Are you sure?" he asked. Her expression was blank, but her entire body was tense, and the last thing he wanted to do was subject her to the fundraising crowd. "Everyone is going to ask you how we know each other and want to make small talk. Are you up for that?"

Her steely gaze leveled him. "It's fine. I can handle a little small talk."

"Of course you can," he started, but before he could get the rest of the words out, she was already out of the truck and headed toward the Victorian.

CHAPTER 24

*L*una strode into the great room of the Victorian, ready to spit fire. Just who did Chad Garber think he was anyway? In the matter of five minutes, he'd managed to turn a hopeful night into one she wished she could forget forever. He'd spied on her. Lied to her. And treated her like… what?

Like she was helpless? No. He definitely hadn't done that. If he'd thought she was helpless, he'd have done far more than just hand her a pile of cash. No, he'd treated her like she needed some help. Which she had.

She could still remember the pure, raw emotion of the day when she'd walked out of juvy. At eighteen years old, she was free of jail and foster care, with a few hundred bucks in her pocket and an address to a group home if she'd needed it. She'd absolutely intended on going to the group home, just until she could get a job and figure out a better living situation. But then the woman with long black hair and earrings lining one entire ear had shown up out of nowhere, claiming to be a private courier with a box for her.

Luna had taken the box and found the cash. It was exactly two hundred dollars more than the amount that Pam had taken from her.

There hadn't been any question what she should do next. She took off, heading north, found a room to rent when the short-term lease was up, and went to work at another coffee shop. There'd never been a reason to look back. Leo and Pam had become people from her past that seemed almost unreal after a while.

Had Chad given her that gift? The money he'd given her that day had absolutely changed her life. Shouldn't she be thanking him for looking after her instead of giving him the cold shoulder? Logically, her head knew he'd probably given her the greatest gift of her life. But her heart? It felt broken that he'd done everything in silence. Her pride was bruised, and she was embarrassed that he'd known just how broken her life had been. That he'd kept tabs on her and never reached out. Why?

Had he known she'd moved to Eureka before he'd come back to Keating Hollow? A weird mix of excitement and dread settled over her at the thought. Guh! What was wrong with her? Why did it make her giddy to think he'd moved there for her while simultaneously pissing her off that he might've been watching her every move the past three years?

"Good evening," a woman in a long black velvet dress said. "Welcome to the Lost Coast Youth Gala."

"Good evening," Luna said, giving the woman her attention.

"Do you have a table assignment yet?"

"Luna is with me," Chad said from behind her. He stopped and held his hand out to the woman. "How's it going, Fiona? Looks like a good turnout."

"Oh, Chad. Hello." Fiona shook his hand and then turned to Luna. "It's lovely to meet you."

"You, too," Luna mumbled, watching as Fiona smiled up at Chad, her eyes sparkling with interest.

"Everyone is dying to hear you play, Chad," Fiona said, maneuvering so that she could slip her arm through his. She snuggled up to him and placed her head on his shoulder. "Thank you so much for doing this. You have no idea how much I appreciate it."

"I'm happy to," he said, glancing over at Luna.

Luna had an intense desire to tug Chad away from the gorgeous woman. Instead, she wrapped her arms around herself, just so that she wouldn't make a scene.

"This way, Chad," Fiona said. "I want you to meet some people."

Chad's jaw clenched, and Luna had the distinct impression that he didn't care for the woman that much. "Just a sec." He reached out a hand to Luna.

She stared at it for a moment.

Chad's deep blue eyes met hers, and she saw a whole host of emotions there, not the least of which was regret.

Dammit. She didn't want him to feel that way. Luna was aware enough to understand that most of her emotions had to do with her own insecurities, and Chad didn't deserve to be shunned just for trying to help her get past a terrible time in her life... even if he had stayed silent. It wasn't what she preferred, and they'd have to have a heart to heart about transparency and trust going forward, but it wasn't as if he'd betrayed her. In fact, up until she met Lincoln Townsend, Chad had been the one and only person who'd cared for her unconditionally since she'd lost her adoptive mom over fifteen years ago.

Forcing herself to relax, she reached out and slipped her hand into his. Chad's fingers instantly tightened over hers, and he pulled her closer as he disengaged from Fiona's clutches.

"Okay, lead on, Fiona. Who is it you want us to meet?" Chad asked.

The host of the event frowned, looking put out, but she caught herself almost instantly and pasted on a smile. "This way. The Dantons gifted the foundation with a substantial amount. Their only request was to meet the man with magic fingers. The wife is a huge fan of classical music. She's heard you play a number of times."

Chad gave the woman a polite smile, but squeezed Luna's hand. She didn't miss the anxiety that flashed in his eyes. Magic fingers indeed. She wondered how much pain he'd be in while trying to get through the performance. Knowing him, she knew he'd give it everything he had and end up with a claw hand again. She squeezed back and focused on the muscles in his palm, sending a tiny bit of her magic over his skin.

He let out a small contented sigh and mouthed, *Thank you.*

She stepped closer to him and whispered, "You're welcome."

Fiona led them around the room, anxious to introduce Chad to all of the wealthy patrons who were there to support the youth center. She was charming and witty with all the guests, the perfect person for getting people to open their wallets. The one thing she was not good at was remembering Luna's name. Fiona introduced her as Lana, Linette, and even Nona at one point. After a while, Luna just found it comical, but by the fourth butchering of Luna's name, Chad lost his cool.

"It's Luna," he huffed out, wrapping his arm around her

shoulders and pulling her into him. He smelled of soap and redwoods and pure sunshine. Luna took in a deep breath and felt the last of her irritation with him disappear.

"Oh, sorry. I'm just so bad at names sometimes," Fiona said with a fake laugh.

"Not when they are attached to four-figure checks," he muttered. But then he pasted a smile on, shook the hand of the man they'd just been introduced to, and then said, "It was nice to meet you again Mr. Xing. If you'll excuse us, I need to find Luna a seat and then get warmed up for the performance."

"Of course. We're looking forward to hearing you play again, Mr. Garber."

"This way," Chad said, leading Luna through the crowd. He kept a tight grip on her hand, not even letting go when they made their way into a small office. Chad sat down in an arm chair and tugged her down to sit sideways on his lap.

"Don't you have to play soon?" she asked, laughing as she leaned into his chest.

"Yes, but I just needed a minute to get away from Fiona and her too important friends." He tilted his head back and closed his eyes. "I'm so sorry about that. Fiona can be such a snob."

"I'm not sure it was snobbery that had her acting like I was a second-class citizen," she said softly, her free hand itching to touch his masculine jawline. "She has a thing for the evening's pianist."

His eyes flew open. "No, she doesn't."

"Yeah, she does." Luna knew they needed to talk, get a few things straight, but she couldn't help herself. She stared at his lips, dying to taste them. "But too bad for her, you're already taken."

Surprise flashed in his gorgeous eyes as he studied her face, drinking her in as if he couldn't quite believe what she'd just said. "I am?"

"Yeah, you are," she said softly and leaned in. His lips were soft and warm under hers as one of his hands gripped her hip. His touch was everything. She wanted to shift her body, to straddle him, and to press her hands to his cheeks and kiss him like she really meant it. But there would be time for that later. Right in that moment, there were things to be said. She pulled back, putting a little distance between them. "I'm not saying I'm happy about how you went about trying to help me three years ago, but I am saying thank you. Your actions probably saved me from a life I was desperate to get away from, and I have no idea how I'm going to repay you for that, but I will."

"Repay me?" he asked, astonished. Then his expression turned serious as he added, "No, Luna. There's no reason to repay me for anything. What you're doing for Levi right now, that's all I could ask for."

"Pay it forward, huh?" She ran her fingers over his jawline, finally giving in to the temptation.

"Yes. And that's exactly what I did, too." He wrapped his arms around her tighter and pulled her closer, brushing his lips over her cheek. "It's not a mystery as to why I was so compelled to help you back then, Luna. My home life with my stepfather was... not good. My mom refused to see it, and the only reason I got out is because a teacher went to bat for me and helped me get into a school that took me out of that situation."

Luna's stomach dropped. "Your stepfather was abusive?"

He nodded. "My mom had full custody, and while I was allowed to visit my father, he and Barb weren't exactly stable back then. He was a musician and she was an artist. They moved around a lot. Living with them wasn't an easy solution, though I'm sure if I'd had the courage to tell Dad what was going on, he'd have moved heaven and earth to get me out of there. It's just…" He shook his head. "Kids don't always think rationally about stuff."

"It's not your fault," Luna said, her voice earnest. "You hear me, Chad. It was never your fault."

He nodded. "Logically, I know that. I just wish I'd known then what I know now."

She wrapped her arms around him and held on tight. "You were a kid."

"Yeah." He pressed his face into her neck and placed a light kiss just below her ear. "So were you."

Luna felt tears prickle the backs of her eyes. She wanted to cry for Chad, herself, for Levi, for all the kids that were suffering because the adults in their lives were shitty people. But instead she just said, "Thank you for being there for me when I needed you, for doing what you did, even though it hurts my pride, and for doing something when no one else would."

"I'd do anything for you, Luna," he said. "Then and now. Always."

A tiny sob got caught in her throat as she forced out, "Call me Hope."

He pulled back and stared into her eyes. "Are you sure?"

"Yes."

He leaned in, his lips barely brushing over hers as he said, "You have no idea how happy that makes me, Hope."

She kissed him softly and tugged him closer for another long hug. And when they finally broke apart, she took his injured hand in hers and started to massage, sending her magic to all of his aches and pains.

"Damn, that feels incredible," Chad said letting out a small moan. "Thank you."

She grinned at him. "If you're going to wow all those rich patrons into opening up their wallets, you'll need to be at the top of your game."

CHAPTER 25

*C*had sat at the piano, his hands gliding easily over the keys. The massage Hope had given him, combined with her healing touch, had been pure magic. His injured hand almost felt just as it had before the altercation with Leo. There was a slight bit of tightness, but nothing to hinder him while he played the two pieces he'd promised the organizers. The first one was a fast, fun number that had the guests stomping and clapping along. The second was haunting and full of emotions. The music rolled through him, taking him over as he slid into that place where nothing else mattered. Only the music.

By the time the last note sounded, Chad was vibrating with pure elation. He hadn't expected to feel that way while playing again, not with his hand so messed up. But he'd forgotten all about his injury, the fact that he no longer played with a company, or that his life had taken a dramatic turn. His joy for music had returned in full force, and he had one person to thank—Hope.

He sat at the piano, scanning the crowd, looking for the

one woman he cared about. Patrons were crowding the piano, already clapping as he reached the crescendo of the piece. His fingers pounded on the keys, releasing a dramatic finish. The crowd erupted with whistles and cheers. Chad stood, craning his neck for a glimpse of Hope. Where was she?

Fiona strode forward, her arms reaching for him, but then his phone buzzed in his pocket. He quickly grabbed it and spotted a text from Hope.

Levi's in trouble. I have to go now. I'm calling a cab. Sorry. You were wonderful.

"Chad, you were amazing!" Fiona said, finally catching up to him and wrapping her arms around him.

He quickly stepped back out of her embrace. "Excuse me." Chad turned and headed straight for the door already tapping out a message.

"Chad! Wait!" Fiona ran after him. "You can't leave. The patrons want to congratulate you on your epic performance."

He barely cast her a glance as he said, "Sorry, Fiona. Family emergency. I have to go."

"But—"

Chad didn't wait around to find out what she was going to say. After hitting send on his message to Hope, he broke out into a jog and headed straight for his truck. He breathed a sigh of relief when he found Hope already standing next to his truck. Her expression was pinched and full of worry. He quickly pulled her into a hug. "What happened?"

Hope's arms tightened around him, but she quickly let go. "I'll tell you on the way. Let's go."

Chad hit the Unlock button on the key fob and ran around to the driver's side. Once they were on the road, he glanced over at her. "Is Levi all right?"

"Physically, I think so." She pressed a button on her phone and frowned. "His uncle showed up looking for him tonight."

"In Keating Hollow?" Chad asked, his grip tightening on the wheel.

"Yeah. Said he needed him to come work for him, and if he didn't, he was going to report him as a runaway."

"That son of a bitch," Chad growled.

"Right." Hope pressed a shaky hand to her throat. "The altercation happened down by the river. Levi said Shannon was there and used her magic to knock his uncle on his ass, giving them enough time to get away. They're at her house, waiting for us."

"He messed with Shannon, too?" Chad asked, grinding his teeth together.

"Apparently. Brian Knox was there too and got into a physical altercation with Levi's uncle when he wouldn't leave Levi alone. Shannon stopped it," Hope said, tapping out a message on her phone. "Levi is being vague on details. I don't know much more than that."

"Brian Knox is who again?" Chad frowned, trying to place the man.

"He's a friend of Jacob Burton. Jacob and Yvette Townsend are engaged."

Chad pressed his foot harder onto the gas pedal, speeding up. The idea that someone had gotten to Levi the one night they'd left town had his stomach rolling with nausea. He swallowed hard. "Got it. It's lucky they were there to help."

"Yeah."

They were both silent for the rest of the thirty-minute drive until they got to town and Hope directed him toward Shannon's house. She lived in a small white cottage that had a lush garden in the front. Moonlight illuminated the flower beds, showing off an impressive assortment of blooms. Chad strode up the curvy path to the front door, but before he could knock, the door swung open and a tall, dark-haired man stepped out, closing the door behind him.

"Brian!" Hope said, pushing past Chad to get to the man. "What happened?"

The man shoved his hands in his pockets and blew out a breath. The porch light suddenly came on, and there was no way to miss Brian's swollen black eye.

"Levi's all right," Brian said. "He's just a little roughed up, nothing too serious. The kids that were with him are unharmed."

"A little bit roughed up?" Hope glanced at the window, clearly itching to run inside.

Chad touched his own eye. "Did Levi's uncle do that?"

Brian nodded. "Shannon and I were just out for a walk when we spotted the man cornering Levi." He glanced at Hope. "Levi says it was his uncle and that he isn't exactly an upstanding citizen."

"That's right," Hope said. "What did he do?"

"When we approached them, the uncle had Levi up against a tree, one hand on his throat. He was threatening to... uh, mess with Candy and Axel if Levi didn't go with him."

Hope's face paled. "But you and Shannon ran him off?"

"We restrained him until Drew could get there, but after Drew cuffed him, the guy still managed to escape his restraints, and he disappeared through the trees. Drew launched a search, but they haven't found him yet."

"Drew knows?" Hope sent Chad a panicked glance, and he knew she was worried about what was going to happen with Levi now. Would he call Child Protective Services? If so, hopefully Lorna could help make sure he wasn't sent anywhere.

"I need to see Levi," Hope said. "Is there anything else I need to know?"

Brian shook his head, and Hope darted into the house.

"Thanks, man. I'm Chad Garber, the new guy who's opening a music store in town," Chad said, holding his hand out. "We appreciate your help."

"Anytime, and nice to meet you. Brian Knox." Brian gave him an appraising glance. "Isn't Levi staying with Luna?"

"Yes, but we're both keeping an eye on him," Chad confirmed.

"I see." Brian glanced back at the door and then at Chad again. "Are you and Luna... a thing?"

Chad didn't exactly know how to answer that. They hadn't defined anything, but even as he admitted that fact to himself, he nodded. "We're dating."

"Lucky man." Brian clapped a hand on Chad's back then glanced back at the house. "The kids are a little shaken up but otherwise all right. I've already given a statement to Drew, but let me know if you need anything else, okay?"

"You're taking off?" Chad asked.

Brian's brow wrinkled, and his lips pressed into a thin line as he stared at the front door. "I need to get home. I think Shannon's probably had enough of me, besides, I have a date with Skye early in the morning."

"Skye?" Chad asked. The name sounded familiar, but he couldn't put a face to it. "Who's that? Someone from Eureka?"

He chuckled. "No. Skye is my buddy Jacob's daughter. He and Yvette have plans, so I get the pleasure of tea parties and maybe a drum lesson."

"Drum lessons?" Chad said with a bark of laughter. "I bet Jacob loves that."

Brian snorted. "There may have been threats to my life, but I'm willing to risk it. Skye's not really old enough yet to do anything but make noise, but her face lights up when she's banging away on her miniature drum set. Besides, the kit is at my house, so they really don't have an argument."

"Sounds headache inducing," Chad said, still smiling.

"Nah. I've been drumming my whole life. Doesn't bother me." Brian waved as he made his way to the street where his SUV was waiting.

Chad watched the man go, wondering what he meant when he'd said Shannon had probably had enough of him. Had he missed something there? He shook his head and stepped into the tiny house. He found Hope sitting at a small dining room table with Levi, Candy, and another boy about their age.

Levi's face was red and his eyes fiery as he ranted about his uncle and how the man had threatened his new friends. "It's one thing for him to come after me, but Candy and Axel are off limits. If Brian and Shannon hadn't shown up when they did…" A small shudder ran through his gangly body.

"I think Levi would've ripped his head off," Candy said, staring at her new friend with a mix of awe and fear. "He was really, really pissed."

"Yeah, he was," the kid who had to be Axel said. He had curly blond hair and was wearing an expression that resembled something more like pride. "I wish I had that kind of confidence when I'm being pushed around." Axel reached out and squeezed Levi's hand briefly before pulling his own hand back.

Chad didn't miss the tiny smile that flashed on Levi's face for just a second before it vanished again. Ah, so Axel was the kid Candy had wanted to set him up with. Well, that part of the evening seemed to have gone as planned at least.

"Everyone okay here?" Chad asked, his gaze landing on Hope.

She gave a tiny nod.

"We're fine," Candy and Axel said at the same time.

"I hate that bastard!" Levi cried as he stood up and buried his hands in his hair. "Why can't he just leave me alone?"

Because you have a special magical gift that's valuable, Chad thought. But he didn't say it. "He will," Chad promised. "We'll get with Lorna and have her file a restraining order. Until then, it's better if you hang out at someone's house just to be safe."

"A restraining order isn't going to keep him away," Levi forced out, his breath catching on the words. His eyes were red and glassy with tears.

Hope stood and wrapped an arm around his shoulders, pulling him away from the other two. They whispered softly as Hope did her best to soothe him.

"Shannon," Chad said, moving into her kitchen where she leaned against the counter. "Thank you for what you and Brian did tonight."

"There's nothing to thank me for. That jackhole deserves to be in jail. I hope Drew tracks him down and makes him suffer."

Candy and Axel nodded.

Levi froze.

Hope whispered something to him, and he shook his head. She sighed and turned around. "I think it's time to call it a night. Candy, Axel, can we give you a ride?"

They looked at each other, but before they could get a word out, Shannon said, "I have to run back into town. I'll take them."

"All right." Hope glanced at Levi. "Ready?"

He nodded and turned to his new friends. "I'm really sorry about tonight. That's not..." He sucked in a breath. "I just wanted to hang out and get to know you better."

"We know," Candy said. "It's not your fault. We can get together in a few days if you want."

"Sunday?" Axel chimed in. "My grandma has a pool. We could go over there."

"That sounds fun," Candy said.

Levi glanced at Hope. "Would that be okay?"

"Of course," she said. "Now let's go home and I'll see what I can do about those bruises."

Levi pressed his hand to his neck, anger flashing in his dark eyes. "Asshole."

Chad had to agree, and he knew that if he ran into the man who called himself Levi's uncle, he'd probably have a hell of a time keeping himself from smashing his other hand into the man's face.

CHAPTER 26

*H*ope watched as Levi paced the living room of her cottage. He was freaking out. There was no other word for it. They'd only been home a half hour when Drew, the town deputy, had shown up on their doorstep. Levi's uncle, Frank Kelley, hadn't been found, though a beat-up, faded-blue truck had been spotted speeding out of town toward the mountains.

"That's him," Levi said. "He's probably headed to one of his buddy's houses out in the sticks. He always disappears out into the country when the heat comes down on him."

Drew made a note. "Do you know any of his buddies or where they live?"

Levi shook his head and continued to pace, his movements jerky. "I can give you the address of the house we stayed at in Eureka. It's not his though."

The deputy wrote down the address.

"Drew," Chad said. "Lorna's on her way. We need to file a restraining order so there's no question this Frank guy shouldn't be near Levi."

Drew sat back in his chair, studying them. "Sure. We can do that. But I have to ask, who has legal custody?"

"We're working on that," Hope said quickly. "Lorna White is—"

"I don't have a legal guardian," Levi spit out. "My dad kicked me out six months ago. I went to stay with my uncle, but they don't talk, and my uncle... Well, he just tried to force me to be a runner for his illegal potions business. So... I'm here. Luna offered me a place to stay and I—" His voice broke, and tears ran unchecked down his face.

Hope's heart shattered right there in her chest. Pain radiated through her and without a thought, she strode over to Levi and wrapped her arms around him. His body shook as he buried his face into her shoulder.

"Okay. I got it." Drew stood and glanced at Chad. "You said Lorna is on her way?"

But before Chad could answer there was a sharp knock on the door. When he opened it, Lorna strode through. She was wearing jeans and a T-shirt, but the white-haired woman was all business as she swung her briefcase onto Hope's table and pulled out papers that were already prepared. "In the state of California, any person twelve and over can file their own orders of protection. Levi, all I need you to do is sign, and we'll have Drew take it from here, all right?"

Levi let go of Hope and nodded. After wiping at his eyes, he picked up the pen and scribbled his signature. "Is that all you need from me?"

"That's it for me," Lorna said.

"I still have a few questions," Drew said.

Levi sent pleading eyes to Hope. She knew he was terrified, but she also knew Drew would do everything in his power to help them. "I think you should talk to Drew. He's only trying to help."

Levi's face was white as he reluctantly nodded.

"Let's go into the living room," Drew said, waving for Levi to precede him. Levi was obviously unhappy about the situation, but he shuffled into the other room with Drew right behind him.

Hope turned to Lorna. "What does this mean? Will Drew have to call Child Protective Services?"

"Not necessarily," the older woman said. "I got confirmation that Levi's father Mike signed for the letter we sent the other day. He hasn't responded yet, but the fact that he knows where his kid is and hasn't even picked up the phone will only help your case. If it comes down to it, we can have Drew call and talk to Levi's dad and try to get verbal confirmation."

Hope's mouth went dry. "What if he says no?"

"Why would he do that?" Chad asked. "He's already made it clear he doesn't want Levi in his house."

"You know as well as I do that people can be evil for no reason at all, Chad," Hope said quietly. "I just don't want to give anyone a chance to hurt Levi again."

"The phone call might be our best option, though," Lorna said. "Why don't we just wait to see what Drew says?"

Hope busied herself in the kitchen, making hot chocolate, while Chad and Lorna sat quietly at the table. It wasn't long before Levi and Drew walked back into the dining room.

Levi hurried into the kitchen and stood next to Hope.

She reached out and grabbed his hand. "You okay?"

"I think so. He wants to call my dad."

Hope closed her eyes and said a silent prayer. "Why?"

"To make sure my story lines up, I guess. I gave him the home number."

Lorna spent the next few minutes filling Drew in on the letter they'd sent to Levi's father.

Drew nodded and excused himself.

"Are you hungry?" Hope asked him.

Levi shook his head. "I've got a headache though."

"Here." She reached up and gently ran her fingers over his temple. Her magic flared to life, and it wasn't long before he let out a sigh.

"Thank you." He leaned against her shoulder and closed his eyes.

Hope wrapped her arms around him, just holding him close. "I've got you, Levi. Don't worry about a thing."

A small tremor went through him and he held on tight, like a small child. Hope wondered if he'd ever had someone to hold like this. The thought brought tears to her eyes as she realized she hadn't had anyone either.

The door creaked open and footsteps sounded on the living room floor as Drew made his way back in. "I have news."

Levi's body stiffened, and then he started to tremble.

"It's okay. Whatever it is, we'll deal with it," Hope murmured.

"I spoke with Mr. Mike Kelley on the phone just now. Levi's father," Drew said. "He's agreed to let Luna take temporary custody."

Hope let out a whoosh of air. "Thank the gods."

Levi's body started to shake as he let out a small sob. Tears soaked Hope's shirt, but she didn't care. She'd hold him for as long as she needed to. She couldn't even imagine how hard it must've been to hear that his own father had given a complete stranger custody. It likely wasn't any harder than being kicked out just for being gay, but it must've ripped open that scab, exposing a gaping wound.

"Thank you, Drew," Hope said, still holding on to Levi.

"Just doing my job," he said. "You'll still need to file with the courts, but since I have the verbal agreement on record and you've already started the paperwork, it shouldn't be an issue. Don't hesitate to give me a call if there's any more trouble. In the meantime, there's still an active manhunt for Frank Kelley. We'll be in touch if and when we find him."

Hope nodded. "We will."

"Good." He mimed a tip of his hat, spun on his heel, and left them to deal with the aftermath of the evening.

Lorna stood, gathered her paperwork, and said, "This is all great news. I'll work on the permanent custody paperwork tomorrow." She stopped near Hope and Levi, her face full of sympathy. "Don't you worry, young man. You're in good hands with Luna and Chad, but they're not the only ones who care about you. I'd dare say the entire town of Keating Hollow is going to be watching over you when they hear about what happened tonight. And a village of witches isn't a group anyone wants to mess with. Not if they don't have a death wish anyway."

Levi lifted his head from Hope's shoulder and glanced at the lawyer. "The entire town?"

Her lips split into a grin. "You're one of us now. Time to get used to it." She lightly patted his arm. "Get some rest. We'll talk more soon."

Levi nodded and wiped at his eyes.

Lorna waved to Hope and mouthed, *Call me tomorrow.*

"I will," Hope said softly.

A moment later, she heard the front door closing, followed by the roar of Lorna's car engine. With the lawyer gone, it was just the three of them again—Chad, Hope, and Levi.

Chad walked over to them, wrapped his arms around both of them, and just held on. "That's the last time anything like that is going to happen to either of you," he said in a low, almost growly voice. "I guarantee it."

Hope closed her eyes, letting his words wash over them, and prayed it was true.

CHAPTER 27

The weekend was low key with Chad, Hope, and Levi hanging out at Hope's house on Saturday. Hope tried to keep Levi's mind off of his uncle by renting a bunch of action movies and settling in for what she would mostly call a guy's day. Chad brought over an outdated Playstation, and the two guys spent a few hours playing a vintage Tony Hawk skateboarding game while Hope baked cupcakes and spent some time weeding the small garden she'd started a few weeks ago. On Sunday, Levi went over to Candy's and spent the afternoon swimming with her and Axel while Hope and Chad spent the afternoon ordering inventory for his music store.

By the time Monday morning rolled around, life had started to feel somewhat normal. Levi's head was mostly healed and he'd get his stitches out in a few days. He seemed settled and even started talking about wanting to go back to high school in the fall. He'd missed an entire semester after being thrown out of his dad's house. Hope made a note to talk to the school to figure out how he could make up the classes.

"We could talk about summer school. I don't think it's

started yet," Hope said as they strode into Incantation Café. "What do you think?"

Levi glanced at his feet and shoved his hands into his pockets.

"What? Are you not ready for that?"

"No, I—" He ran a hand through his dark curls. "I guess I just thought we had to wait for something to be finalized before I could..." Levi shrugged. "I don't know. I feel like I'm in limbo."

"Before you could start to move forward with your life?" Hope guessed.

"Yeah."

She reached over and squeezed his hand. "I get that. I've been there before. It's worse when you start to acclimate and then get the rug pulled out from under you. It's up to you. And I mean that. But I really don't think we're going to have an issue, and it will probably look better to the judge if we show that we mean business. Enrolling you in school is a pretty permanent step."

"You think so?" he asked, his eyes sparking with hope.

"I do. You like school, don't you?" she said with a tilt of her head.

"I didn't used to think so," he said, this time meeting her eyes. "But once I didn't have the option, I realized it was always my way out."

"Out of your dad's house?" she asked.

"Out of everything. His house. That tiny town he lives in. The small minds of the people who live there. I just don't want to end up stuck anywhere."

"I get that," Hope said with a pleased smile. "An education is a powerful thing. And there's a big world outside of Keating Hollow."

"That's not what I meant," Levi said with a frown. "I don't want to leave here. Not now anyway."

She placed a soft hand on his arm. "I know, Levi. Don't worry about that. I want you to have an education and choices. It's what you deserve."

There was silence for a moment before he flashed her a smile. "Thanks."

"Nothing to thank me for," she reassured him before pulling him into a tight hug.

After they had their lattes in hand and a couple of pastries, Hope and Levi met Chad outside on the cobbled sidewalk.

"Good morning to my two favorite people," Chad said, striding up to them, looking at good as ever. His light hair was slightly too long, a lock falling over one eye, and his blue eyes were gleaming with mischief.

"Good morning yourself," Hope said, leaning in for a quick kiss.

Levi nodded at him and took a sip of his latte.

"It's a big day," Chad said. "Levi, are you up for helping me with the store signage today? Our marquee is ready to be hung."

"Of course," Levi said, the troubled expression in his eyes vanishing. It seemed that any time Chad had something physical for the two of them to do that Levi was able to shred his worries if even for just a fraction of time.

"Great. Come with me. We'll let Hope get to work." He turned to her. "Are we on for dinner still?"

"Seven. Sharp," she said. The last two times she'd invited him over, he'd been hopelessly late after losing track of time while working to get the store up and running. "Don't make me wait for my dinner this time."

Chad had enough self-awareness that her statement caused

guilt to creep over his features. He nodded softly. "Yeah. Okay. Got it."

Hope saluted him with her latte and laughed. "We'll see."

"Count on it," Chad promised as he draped an arm around Levi's shoulder and led the kid down to his music store.

She stared at the two men in her life. Just a few weeks earlier, all of her relationships had been at arm's length. Now she had a teenager she'd already fallen for and the one man she'd always wanted. Things were a little stressful with Levi's custody still in limbo, but she wouldn't change any of it for the world. Her heart was full and for the first time in her life, she had people to shower with the love that was bursting from deep inside her. It felt good. Better than good. It felt downright perfect.

Smiling to herself, Hope strolled down the street, already working on the night's menu. Levi had proven to be a bottomless pit, as most teenage boys were. That was perfectly fine. It gave her an excuse to make all her favorite pasta dishes. Tonight, she decided, would be manicotti. Her mouth watered just thinking about it. She was just about to reach for the door to the spa when a man behind her said, "Why, if it isn't Hope Scott."

Hope froze, a chill running down her spine. That voice. She'd know it anywhere. What was Leo doing in Keating Hollow? She turned around and glared at her former foster mother's boyfriend. A familiar ache in her gut her stomach turn as she stared at his stringy hair and the dark circles rimming his eyes.

"This town is a little fancy for the likes of you, isn't it?" he taunted.

That rage she'd barely kept in check all the years she'd lived in Pam's house boiled right to the surface, but she managed to keep herself from hauling off and decking the good-for-nothing lowlife. "What do you want, Leo?"

"Levi. You have no business giving that kid a place to live. He belongs with his uncle, with family," he said. "Not with an uppity girl who doesn't even know how to keep herself out of jail."

Despite the bolt of pure outrage that seized her brain, Hope didn't react to his taunts that were aimed at disarming her. Instead she focused on what was most important—Levi. "How do you know Levi and his uncle?"

Leo tsked. "Not that it's any of your business, you ungrateful witch, but Frank is a business associate of mine. And he wants his nephew to come home. Hand him over and I'll leave without another word."

"Or what?" she asked, narrowing her eyes further. There was no chance he didn't already have some plan to make her life hell. It was just a matter of finding out what that might be.

Leo's face turned a dark shade of red as he stalked toward her. "Don't look at me like that, Hope. Like I'm something not even worthy of gracing the bottom of your shoe. I know your history. Remember that. I know everything. What do you think your boss will say when she finds out you're an ex-con?"

"Her boss will tell you to get the hell off her private property," Faith said, appearing out of nowhere right behind Leo.

Panic flared to life in Hope's chest as she wondered exactly how much Faith had heard? Did she hear him say she'd been in juvy?

Faith crossed over arms her chest, and her green eyes flashed with something dangerous. "I don't know who you are, mister, but I don't take kindly to nasty old men threatening my sister. I suggest you step away before our sister Yvette decides to light a fire under your ass."

Hope glanced over Faith's shoulder and spotted her oldest sister, Yvette. The woman had her hands up and flames danced over her palms.

"Move along, jackass," Yvette ordered, tossing her long chestnut hair over one shoulder. "Probably best to do that before Noel gets here. She's not nearly as restrained as Faith and I are. Chances are she'll knock you on your butt and pin you there until her deputy husband arrives and hauls your ass to jail."

He snorted. "For what exactly? Having a conversation with my daughter?"

"Daughter?" Hope snarled, his words snapping her out of her shock of finding two of her sisters coming to her defense. "Have you lost your mind? I am not, nor was I ever, your daughter. You were just sleeping with my foster mom. That makes you nothing to me. Nothing but a bad memory."

"Leave. Now," Yvette said, tossing a ball of fire near the man's feet.

He jumped back, scowled at her, and then turned to Hope. "If you don't send Levi back to his uncle within the next two days, there will be consequences. Count on it."

"Don't think you can threaten me, Leo," Hope said through clenched teeth. "I'm never sending Levi anywhere he doesn't want to go. So do whatever it is you're threatening to do. I don't really care to be honest."

"Cocky," he said under his breath. "We'll just see what your new boyfriend has to say about all of this."

Chad? She let out a bubble of laughter. It didn't matter what this loser of a man said to Chad. He knew all of her secrets already. Nothing he could say to him was of any importance.

Leo was already a good thirty feet away when he glanced back and said, "Laugh it up now. You won't think it's funny when he ends up in jail. But I guess you don't have much of a problem with that considering you know all about what it's like, right, Hope?"

She clenched her fists, vibrating with frustration and anger. She had no doubt that Leo would cause them problems. He was that kind of person. If he couldn't use real dirt, he'd just make something up. She was certain of it. But Chad could take care of himself, and there was no reason on earth other than a court order that could convince her to send Levi back to his uncle. "Get out of here, Leo. I won't be intimidated by you ever again."

Yvette unleashed another fireball, this time coming perilously close to singeing Leo's tattered jeans.

He scowled at her. "I'll put you behind bars, too."

Yvette laughed. "I'd love to see you try."

Leo flipped them off and scurried down the street to a light blue pickup truck. Hadn't Levi's uncle been driving a blue truck? Hope pulled out her phone and called Drew. His phone immediately went to voicemail. "Damn," she muttered while waiting for the tone. After leaving him a message, she turned to her sisters. "Thank you for that."

"No thanks needed. That guy is a major douchecanoe," Yvette said, moving to stand next to Hope. She wrapped an arm around the younger woman's shoulders and pulled her in for a side hug. "He's lucky I didn't burn his junk off."

Faith chortled as she pulled the spa's door open. "That would've been something to see. Flaming balls in downtown Keating Hollow."

"It would certainly give everyone something to talk about." Yvette grinned at Hope. "Not to mention a sense of intense satisfaction at knowing that jackass couldn't procreate anymore."

Hope knew her oldest sister was trying to lighten the mood, but Hope was fixated on the fact that the Keating Hollow residents certainly would have something to talk about now. There was no chance the small altercation this morning with Leo had gone unnoticed. Besides, Faith and Yvette would certainly tell the rest of the family and their significant others. She'd be the talk of the town in no time. It was what she'd been hoping to avoid, but she should know better than anyone that she couldn't outrun her past.

"Listen," Hope said. "About that thing he said about me being in jail—"

"Let's talk in my office," Faith said, cutting her off. She held the door open and waved the other two women in.

"Well, good morning," Lena said. "I was wondering when you were finally going to get a move on. Abby and Noel are already in your office."

"Thanks, Lena," Faith said, already striding toward the hallway. She opened the door and looked at Hope. "After you."

Hope's gaze swiveled between Yvette and Faith. What was going on here? Some sort of intervention? Had her four sisters gotten together to try to convince her to stay away from their father? Or to leave town so she didn't disrupt their perfect lives? Her heart sank as she imagined the worst. But hadn't Yvette just threatened to permanently maim Leo on her behalf? And although Faith hadn't threatened bodily harm, she'd certainly stood up for Hope when it came to Leo. Maybe Hope was jumping to conclusions. It wouldn't hurt to hear them out, though she would've preferred to have had some sort of advanced notice she was meeting with all four of her sisters. At the very least she could have steeled herself for any number of scenarios. Instead, she was raw after her confrontation with Leo and felt blindsided by the meeting.

"Luna?" Yvette asked. "Are you all right?"

Hope sucked in a fortifying breath. "Yeah. Sorry. Just still trying to recover from the shock of Leo showing up here after all these years." She swept past her two sisters and headed straight for Faith's office.

"There you two are," Noel said, glancing at Faith and Yvette. Even though she was frowning, she glowed and was casually holding her impressive baby bump. Through the grapevine, Hope had learned that she was about seven months pregnant. "I was beginning to think Abby and I had the time wrong."

Abby rolled her eyes. "Please, Noel. They're only five minutes later. Give them a break." She waved at Hope. "Morning, little sis."

"Uh, morning," Hope said, taken off guard by the casual way she'd said *little sis*.

"Okay, before we start, we need to fill you in on an altercation we just had outside the spa," Yvette said. "Some dude was threatening Luna, trying to get her to give up Levi. But I scared him off."

"Yeah, she threatened to burn his balls off," Faith said, taking a seat on the couch. She turned her attention to Hope. "But I'm a little unclear on what was happening there. Luna, do you mind filling us in?"

Hope paced the room, her insides churning with anxiety. She didn't want to talk about this, but she really had no choice. These women had stood by her and deserved to know what they'd just stepped in. "Leo is the boyfriend of my former foster mom. They make and sell potions, or at least did when I was still in Pam's care."

"No," Abby said, her hand rising to cover her mouth. "That's awful."

"Yeah, it was," Hope confirmed, unable to ignore the way Faith's eyes narrowed slightly. "Anyway, I haven't seen either of them in over three years. I had no idea he was here in Keating Hollow until ten minutes ago, or even in Humboldt county. We lived in Berkeley. Anyway, he just showed up demanding I hand over Levi to Levi's uncle, Frank Kelley, which leads me to believe that Leo is partnering with Levi's uncle, Frank Kelley, since he too is involved in illegal potions."

"That's quite the coincidence," Faith said. "That Leo would be working with Levi's uncle, don't you think?"

"Oh, come on, Faith," Abby said, frowning at her sister. "You know that the illegal potions trade is fairly small. I'd be more surprised if the two didn't know each other." She gave her head a little shake and turned to Hope. "Whatever you need, you let me know. I'm one hundred percent behind you, little sis."

Hope's heart swelled at Abby's complete acceptance, but she knew she had more to explain. If she was going to forge a relationship with any of these women, she wanted all of her secrets out in the open. "Thank you for that. But there's something else you should know."

All four sisters were silent as they waited for her to continue. They were a study in contrasts, and yet, all had familiar features that just screamed 'sisters.' Noel's blond hair had been been cut short again while Yvette's natural chestnut locks shone with blond highlights. While Abby and Faith both had long blond hair, Faith was dressed neatly in a floral skirt and a formfitting T-shirt while Abby had on grungy beige capri pants and a stained T-shirt. She'd obviously come from her potions studio where she made energy potions and magically infused high-end body soaps and lotions.

Hope glanced away and her voice cracked as she said, "I spent almost three months in juvy for selling illegal potions three years ago."

"When you were seventeen?" Noel asked. There was something raw in her voice that had Hope giving her sister her full attention. Noel's expression had been neutral, but now it was stormy as she kept her blue eyes locked on Hope. "Did your foster mom know about that?"

"She's the one who forced me to do it," Hope said. "She ah… stole the money I was saving for college and said she'd give it back only if I made the run for her and collected the payment."

All four of her sisters cried out their protests at such an injustice. The four of them closed ranks around her, hugging her while Faith cursed their mother Gabby for putting Luna in that position in the first place. Hope spent the next half hour filling them in on her history, starting with her adoptive mom and her death, and then she spoke briefly about the foster homes she'd been in. By the time she got to Chad, Abby was crying softly, and Noel looked like she wanted to murder someone. Yvette kept soothing her by running her hand up and down Hope's back. But Faith had stepped away and was now pacing the office.

"Faith?" Yvette asked. "What's going on in that head of yours?"

Hope was overwhelmed with the unconditional support three of her sisters had bestowed upon her. She hadn't quite figured Faith out, but understood that of the four of them, she was the most cautious.

Faith stopped her pacing. "I have a few questions. One major one, really."

"Okay," Hope said, trying to settle the nerves in her stomach. She didn't know why she was nervous exactly. She'd already spilled all of her secrets. Now she just wanted a place in this family that she'd never dreamed she deserved.

"Why did Leo call you Hope?" she asked.

"Oh. That's the name our mother gave me. After juvy... I changed it to Luna. You know, as a fresh start. A way to distance myself from that life. But recently I've realized that I can't keep running from who I was back then and have decided to go back to Hope. I know it's confusing, but you can call me by either name."

"Our mother named you Hope?" Abby said, her eyes wide.

"Yeah," Hope said with a humorless chuckle. "Ironic, huh?"

"I think it's perfect." Abby wrapped her arms around Hope and held on tight. "It suits you."

Yvette joined the hug, while Noel went to Faith and grabbed her hand. "I think we've had our questions answered, Faith," Noel said softly.

But Faith shook her head. "No. I have one more."

"Okay." Hope stepped out of Abby's and Yvette's embrace. "Lay it on me."

Faith closed her eyes for just a moment. When she opened them, she sent Hope a small smile. "Will you come to dinner at Dad's tomorrow night? I think it's about time we welcome you to the family. You're welcome to bring Levi and Chad if you want to."

Something warm and unfamiliar flooded Hope's system. Tears stung her eyes as she nodded. "I'd love to."

CHAPTER 28

C had sat across from Hope at Woodlines, gazing at her smiling face. Her eyes sparkled with a happiness he'd never known her to have when she was a teenager, and he found himself wanting to spend the rest of his life making sure that look never faded.

"What are you staring at?" she asked as she lowered her menu to the table.

"The most beautiful woman I've ever seen."

Her face turned a sweet shade of pink even as she rolled her eyes. "That's a sweet thing to say, but hardly original. You can do better than that."

He laughed. "Nah. I'm too dazzled by that sparkle in your eye to come up with anything other than clichés."

She snorted. "Okay, Mr. Sweet Talker. But next time I expect a little more effort."

Chad reached across the table and took her hand, lightly stroking the pad of his thumb over her palm. "You just seem really happy. It's a good look on you."

"I am happy," she confirmed. A slow smile claimed her lips. "A lot of that is thanks to you."

It was also thanks to the fact that the Townsend family had embraced her as one of their own and that a judge had officially granted her temporary custody of Levi. Thankfully, Leo hadn't been back, and the shock of his appearance a few weeks ago had started to fade into the background. Life had finally fallen into place for Hope. And Chad was just happy to be a part of it. In fact, he was hoping to someday become a permanent part of it. But it was way too soon to be asking that important question, so instead he asked, "What do you think about making this relationship exclusive?"

Hope tilted her head to one side and studied him, her lips twitching with amusement. "Did you think I was looking to troll the dating sites for a little variety?"

Chad laughed, unable to even picture such a thing. Dating sites weren't Hope's style. "No. I just wanted to make it official. Let you know I'm all-in on this."

Her expression softened, and her hand tightened around his as joy radiated from her bright green eyes. "In that case, I think exclusive sounds wonderful. Does that mean I get to call you my boyfriend?"

"I'm counting on it," he said, his voice husky with emotion. Then he leaned across the table and brushed his lips over hers. His heart sped up, and warmth filled him all the way to his toes. And for the first time in his life, he was willing to name the emotion that was sweeping through him... Love. He was in love with the woman sitting across from him. He didn't know when it had happened. Not back in Berkeley. He'd never thought of her like that. Maybe he'd fallen that first day he saw her sitting at the Townsend's brewery looking so lovely that his insides had turned to goo. Or maybe it was the day she'd let him help her move and she'd been ready and willing to do anything she could to help Levi. He didn't know. But it was more than clear to him that she owned his heart now, and he wanted to give her anything and everything he had.

A long shadow fell over their table, and Chad glanced up to find the deputy sheriff looking down at him with a pained expression.

"Drew. What's wrong?" Hope asked.

"I'm really sorry to be interrupting your dinner, but I'm here on official business." He held a piece of paper out to Chad. "It's a warrant for your arrest for assaulting Leonardo Mahoney."

Hope let out a gasp while Chad groaned.

"That son of a…" Hope spat out. "This is garbage. Chad never assaulted him. You can't—"

"Hope," Chad said, cutting her off by raising his injured hand.

She clamped her mouth shut and stared at two fingers that were now slightly crooked, and he knew she understood.

Chad handed Hope his truck keys and threw a few bills on the table as he stood. "Drew is just doing his job." He turned to the deputy. "Do you have to cuff me? I'm willing to go with you to the station so we can straighten this out."

"I don't see why if you're not resisting," Drew said, rolling his shoulders as his facial features relaxed.

"I'm not," Chad said with a resigned sigh. There hadn't been any witnesses that night of the altercation with Leo. Chad had been willing to let it go, but now it was clear he'd just been stupid.

Hope stood, too. "I'll call Lorna."

"Thanks," Chad said and followed Drew out of the restaurant.

~

"WANT to tell me what happened that night?" Drew asked Chad.

They were sitting at a metal table in the town's small police station. Lorna was to the right of Chad already scribbling notes. She'd come right away after Hope's phone call, and she and Chad had spoken for about ten minutes before they sat down with Drew.

Chad glanced at Lorna.

The lawyer nodded. "Just the facts, Chad. No need to elaborate."

"All right." Chad flexed his hand, the muscles and tendons aching with just the memory. "I'd just gotten out of my Uber and was headed to my Airbnb after a performance in San Francisco on the night of the incident, when Leo popped up out of nowhere and swung at me. He clocked me in the temple, and I went down sideways, twisting my knee. Then he was on me, fists flying. But I managed to roll and get the upper hand, and when I saw who it was, I just lost it. Before I knew it, I was pummeling him with my right fist. Unfortunately, he twisted out of my grip and the last blow hit the pavement, breaking multiple bones and ending my career as a professional pianist."

Drew scribbled down Chad's story, his lips pursed in concentration.

Chad leaned back in his chair, trying to calm the nerves in his gut. He'd thought he had nothing to be worried about. Leo had taken the first swing. He was also the type of guy who didn't like to involve the police in his business, so Chad hadn't ever imagined he'd go to the police. If he'd known that, he would've made his own police report. Instead, he'd just gone to the hospital, gotten his hand taken care of, and then dealt with the ramifications of trying to crush the man's skull in. He wasn't proud of the way he'd lost control, but he wasn't exactly ashamed either. Leo was a grade-A douche.

"So, Leo attacked you first?" Drew asked.

"Yes," Chad said.

"Did you report it?"

"No." Chad glanced down at his hand. Hell, he should've reported it. At least there'd have been an official record.

"Why?" Drew asked.

Chad shrugged. "I didn't think it would matter to be honest. I couldn't sue the bastard for the destruction of my career. He doesn't have anything. And in San Francisco the police have a lot more to deal with than a one-off altercation. I just wanted to figure out how to get my life back together. Dealing with police reports just seemed like more effort than it was worth."

Drew tsked but didn't comment. He ran through a series of more questions, asking about Leo's motives and why the man targeted him. Chad answered as best he could, but he didn't know the answers himself. All Leo had said was that he knew what Chad had done and he was going to pay the price. Chad assumed he meant the money he'd given Hope to get away from Leo and Pam, but he couldn't be sure.

"Okay, well, I have to book you," Drew said. "I don't have a choice. But if you have the cash you can bond out immediately." He rattled off the amount.

Chad nodded. "I can do that. Not a problem."

"Good. I'd hate to see you behind bars even if you had taken the first swing. This guy has a record a mile long." He grinned at Lorna. "Forget I said that."

"I didn't hear a thing," the lawyer said.

Twenty minutes later, Chad walked out of the sheriff's office and headed straight for Hope's house.

CHAPTER 29

ope was so angry she was ready to scratch Leo's eyes out with her bare fingernails. After she paid the bill at Woodlines, she grabbed Chad's keys and intended to head to the station to wait for him. Instead, as she was opening the driver's side door of the truck, a hand came out of nowhere and slammed it shut again.

"What the hell?" she cried as she spun around, adrenaline coursing through her veins. Her startled gaze landed on Leo's beady eyes. "You," she accused. "How dare you show up here after filing assault charges against Chad?"

"That jackass. I should've killed him when I had the chance," Leo said, slurring his words. He crowded her closer to the truck, trapping her between him and the door. "I thought for sure that sucker punch to the head would do enough damage to keep him down while I explained to him exactly why he deserved to have his ass beat. Little effer had more fight in him than I realized."

So, he *had* thrown the first punch. Hope figured as much.

Chad wasn't the type to go around picking fights if he didn't have to. "Go away, Leo. You're not welcome here."

He threw his head back and laughed. "I don't think so. Not until you give me the kid."

"Why? What is it you need him for? Do you work with his uncle or something?" she asked, just to keep him talking. If she kept him distracted, maybe she'd have an opening to get safely into the truck.

"I owe Frank a debt. He's willing to forgive it if I bring his nephew back to him. So do your duty to the one who raised you and take me to him. Or else you're going to find out what happens when you defy the man of the house." He thrust his hips suggestively, making her stomach roll.

She chose to ignore his taunts about raising her and being the man of the house. Neither of those statements were based in reality. But then, he appeared to be so high that likely most of what he was saying probably wasn't based in reality either. "Levi filed a restraining order against Frank. Even if I was inclined to agree with your insane demands, it isn't going to change anything. Frank can't be within 100 yards of him anyway."

"Pfft." Leo waved an impatient hand. "No one cares about any damned restraining order. Where Frank is taking him that won't be an issue."

Hope wanted to gag at his words. He was such a vile human being she wondered if he'd ever had any redeeming qualities. If so, she'd never seen any of them. Not that she cared. All she wanted to do was get the hell away from him and make sure Levi was safe. He'd gone to Candy's house earlier in the evening and was due home any minute now. The thought of him home alone sent a shot of fear through her. What if Frank was just waiting for him and tried to snatch him again? She pressed both palms to Leo's chest and pushed as hard as she could.

The man stumbled backward, and Hope quickly pulled the truck door open again. But before she could climb in, he grabbed her arm and twisted, sending her straight to her knees. "Don't you ever put your hands on me, girly," he snarled. "Do that again and I'll break all of your fingers. Got it?"

"Let her go!" a boy shouted in the dark night.

Hope's breathing stopped altogether as she recognized Levi's voice. *No. No! Go home, Levi!* The words echoed in her head as tears fell down her cheeks because of the pain radiating through her arm.

"Ahh, if it isn't the boy I was looking for all along," Leo said. "Frank's found you a nice man to take care of all your needs, Levi. Doesn't that sound nice? Just because your daddy doesn't care for your orientation it doesn't mean Frank has a problem with it. In fact, I'm pretty sure that sugar daddy he's found will make sure you have everything you need just as long as you behave and do what we say."

Levi's face blanched in the pale moonlight.

Hope was sure she was going to vomit. "You disgusting pig," Hope ground out. "Levi is never going with you. Got it? Not if I have anything to say about it."

"Oh no?" Leo yanked on her arm so hard a scream ripped from her throat. But it was nothing compared to the foot that landed on her ribs.

"Stop! Stop!" Levi cried, frantic now. "I'll go with you. Just stop hurting her."

"At least one of you has some sense," Leo said. He nodded to Levi and then to the blue truck a few spaces away. "Get in the truck."

"Let her go first," Levi demanded.

"Want me to break another rib?" he asked.

Levi's mouth dropped open as he shook his head.

"Good. Then get in the truck."

"Not so fast," another voice called. This one was high-pitched and full of fury. "I told you I'd burn your junk off if you came near her again."

Yvette. Pure relief rushed through Hope. Her sister would never let Levi go with Leo. No matter what happened, he'd be safe.

Leo stiffened then yanked Hope up to her feet, wrapped an arm around her neck, and squeezed, blocking her airway. "Back off, witch. Do it, or I'll kill her."

"I'd like to see you try," Noel said, emerging from the shadows, wind swirling around her and making her hair lift from the force of it. Faith, Abby, and Hanna rounded out the group. The five women formed a half circle around Hope and Leo, each of them tapping their magic in terrifying ways. Faith and Hanna, the two water witches, had both produced thick, pointy icicles that were aimed right at Leo's skull. Abby had her hand aimed at one of the planter boxes on the sidewalk where a vine was growing rapidly and inching toward Leo.

"Let her go, or things are going to get really ugly for you really quickly," Yvette ordered.

Leo jerked Hope to the right, trying to put her in the path of the icicles, but the moment that happened they shifted, this time pointing at his exposed groin. He jerked Hope to the left, trying to cover himself, but Abby's vine reached his ankle and quickly wrapped itself around his leg. She snapped her fingers, and the vine instantly pulled back, sending Leo to his butt. He didn't let go of Hope, and she went down with him. But the leverage of his grip was compromised, and she was able to quickly squirm out of his grip.

Then all hell broke loose. All five witches unleashed their magic, pelting Leo. Noel's wind held him down while Yvette's fire flamed to life around him, leaving him no way to run off without breaching the flames. Abby's vines quickly worked to hogtie the man in place. Hanna's and Faith's icicles melted from the fire, but it didn't matter. Leo was contained and wasn't going anywhere anytime soon.

Levi ran into Hope's arms, burying his face in her neck. "I'm so sorry," he muttered over and over again. "It's my fault this happened. I'm sorry. I'm so sorry."

"Shhh," she whispered into his ear. "It's not your fault. Don't ever think that. It's Leo and Frank's fault. And your dad's fault for being so closeminded. But never your fault. You didn't cause any of this, all right?"

Levi shook his head, unable to accept that he was the victim.

"Please, Levi. Look at me." She pulled back just far enough so that she could stare into his dark eyes. "Say it. It's not my fault."

He shook his head. "If I hadn't called Chad that night. If I'd just…" Tears leaked from his eyes, and he let out a sob.

"I'm glad you called Chad. You did the right thing. If you hadn't, we wouldn't have found each other. And I don't know about you, kid, but I'm grateful every day that you came into my life. I wouldn't have it any other way. Got that?"

When he didn't respond, she kissed his forehead and whispered, "You deserve to be loved, Levi. I love you. Chad loves you. And it sure looks like my sisters do, too." She glanced over his shoulder at the five women who were standing watch over her, Levi, and the bound man on the pavement.

"I've always wanted a brother," Faith said quietly.

"Me, too," the other three Townsend sisters agreed.

Hope's eyes filled with tears as emotion rippled through her. This was what it meant to be a family. She let the tears roll unchecked down her cheeks as she forced out, "Looks like you're stuck with us, Levi."

His tears came hard and fast as he buried his face in her neck again. And this time as she held him, the Townsend sisters wrapped their arms around the pair while Hanna watched over Leo.

CHAPTER 30

"Need a snack?" Hope asked Levi as she placed a plate of cheese, salami, and crackers on the coffee table. He was sitting on the couch, working his way through a chapter in his algebra book. It had been too late to enroll in summer school, but Hope decided to start him on a homeschool course, and they'd hit the ground running. There was a lot of material to get through before he started classes in the fall.

"Thanks," he said without looking up.

Chad added a large glass of root beer to the coffee table and then tugged Hope back into the kitchen. As soon as they were out of sight, he pressed her against the wall and covered her lips with his. She melted into him.

It had been a week since Leo had been hauled off to jail. One week since her sisters had saved both her and Levi from Leo's wrath. One week since all the charges against Chad had been dropped. Since Levi had overheard Leo confessing to assaulting Chad first, his testimony had been enough for the judge to throw out Leo's complaint. It didn't hurt that Leo's record was a mile long while Chad's was squeaky clean.

"Want to try another date tonight?" Chad asked between kisses. "The last one didn't exactly end the way I planned."

Hope chuckled. "And how was it supposed to end? With me in your bed?"

His eyes flashed with heat. "No, but only because I live in an apartment above my stepmother's garage and am currently making do with a sofa bed until I figure out my housing situation. I was going to do that after I'm done pouring money into the music shop. But if you wanted to invite me into yours…" He grinned. "I won't say no."

Gods. She'd been so close to inviting him to spend the night a couple of times over the past week, but then she'd thought of Levi. And even though she knew he wouldn't care, she'd still hesitated. Life was finally falling into place, and she didn't want to do anything to mess it up. She glanced toward the living room.

Chad's grin faltered, and he nodded solemnly. "I get it. No need to say anything more."

"I'm sorry. I just feel a little strange about it still."

He reached out and brushed a lock of her blond hair out of her eyes. "No need to apologize. Really. But if you want to take a long lunch break sometime this week…"

A shot of desire rippled through her. Levi did have plans to see his friends Axel and Candy on Thursday. And she did have the morning free before she had to head into Eureka to work with Healer Snow. "How about Thursday morning? Ten o'clock? I could make you breakfast and then…" She cleared her throat. "I'm free until about one."

That heat was back in his eyes, and his voice was full of gravel as he said, "It's a date."

Butterflies fluttered in her belly as she thought of stripping him out of his clothes and running her hands all over his beautiful body. His lips came down on hers again, and this time the kiss was slow and sensual, giving her a taste of what was to come in just a few days. Guh, how was she going to wait? She'd wanted him for years. Maybe his sofa bed wasn't a terrible option. She was still contemplating following him home that night when the doorbell rang.

She heard Levi get up and open it, followed by him inviting someone in.

"She's in the kitchen with Chad," Levi said.

"Thanks," the soft-spoken man said.

Chad took a step back, putting space between him and Hope. She moved to stand next to the new kitchen table she'd purchased a few days ago just as Lincoln Townsend entered the room.

"Lin. Hi," she said, smiling at him. "What brings you by today?"

He glanced at Chad and then back at Hope. After clearing his throat, he held up an envelope. "The results from the paternity test came back."

From the look on his face, it didn't look like good news, and Hope dropped into one of the chairs. "You're not my father." Her voice was flat, and an ache had already settled around her heart.

"I'm sorry, sweetheart, but no. I wish with all my heart I was though," he said, sitting across from her and grabbing both of her hands.

Chad moved to stand behind Hope and placed his hands on her shoulders.

"I wish that, too," she said, barely holding back tears. "I can't think of anyone better to fill that role."

"I'm still up for the job," Lincoln said, his blue-gray eyes serious. "Like I said before, this changes nothing for me. You're family. My girls are your sisters, and you're still Gabby's daughter. If she'd have stayed with me, I'd have raised you as my own. I see no reason to not claim you the same way now."

She'd heard him the first time when she'd been out at the Townsend farm. She knew he meant it, too. It was just that she'd wanted this so much. The news was a crushing blow.

"There's something else," Lin said, pulling out another piece of paper. He slid it across the table. "This is your original birth certificate. It lists someone else as your dad."

Hope stared at the paper as if it were a snake that might bite her. "Where... um, where did you get this?"

"From Gabby." He gave her a sympathetic smile. "After I got the results, I called her to find out more information. She was... Well, she was contrite and said she'd been hopeful that you were mine but that she was pretty sure all along that Michael Kelley is your biological father."

That name sounded entirely too familiar to Hope and she frowned, trying to place it.

"What did you just say?" Levi asked from the opening between the living room and the kitchen.

The lightbulb went off over Hope's head, and she let out a gasp as she realized where she'd heard that name.

"Michael Kelley. Why? Do you know him?" Lin asked.

Levi's gaze darted to Hope, and his Adam's apple bobbed as he swallowed hard. "How is that possible?"

Shock had rendered Hope speechless, but as she looked at Levi, the only emotion she felt was pure joy. If they shared a father, then Levi was her half-brother. She was almost afraid to let herself believe that it could be possible. If she was related to Levi, getting permanent custody just got a whole lot easier.

Not to mention, she'd just found out that the kid she already loved was her brother. "I don't really know, Levi, but if it's true, I…" Her voice cracked, and tears welled in her eyes. "I couldn't be happier."

Levi's eyes turned red as he shook his head. "It's too good to be true." He pressed a hand to his heart and closed his eyes. "I'm almost afraid to believe it."

"Levi's father's name is Michael Kelley," Chad whispered to Lin, filling him in.

"Oh. I see," Lin said softly. He dug into his pocket and pulled out a piece of paper. "Here is all the information that Gabby gave me about him. Maybe this will help."

Hope pulled out the chair beside her and gestured for Levi to take a seat. Once he was perched beside her, she grabbed his hand with one of hers and took the piece of paper from Lin with the other. There was an address, dates, and a couple of relatives Gabby remembered meeting in the short time that she and Michael had been together.

"Mindy Kelley," Levi choked out. "She was my grandmother."

Lin nodded. "Gabby said she thought Mindy was either his mom or his aunt. She wasn't sure."

Tears leaked from Levi's eyes. "She was both. She adopted her sister's child after her sister died in a car accident."

Hope let go of the paper Lincoln had given her as she turned to Levi, studying him. Was this why she'd felt such an instant connection to him? She'd always thought it was because they shared a similar past, but could it be the blood connection? It was possible. Either way, her heart was full of joy. Not because she knew who her biological father was. By all accounts, he sounded like a total douche, and she had zero desire to meet him after what he'd done to Levi. No, all of her joy was reserved for the wonderful boy sitting beside her.

Standing, Hope pulled Levi to his feet and wrapped her arms around him. "Welcome home, little brother."

HOPE SAT next to Levi in the county court as the judge adjusted her glasses. Lorna had told them this was all a formality, but still the breath got caught in her throat as she waited to hear the judge's decision regarding Levi's permanent custody. Just out of an abundance of caution, the day Hope had taken Levi to meet with Dr. Snow about his abilities, Hope asked her mentor if she could run a genetic test to prove that they were brother and sister. She'd wanted the results faster than the test she and Lin had taken. Dr. Snow hadn't hesitated. The results had come back as ninety-nine percent certainty that the two were brother and sister. Lorna wasted no time sending the extra information to the judge, and now it was the moment of truth.

"This case has been an interesting one from the start," the judge said, her gaze landing on Hope and Levi. "These two individuals have been through a lot in their relatively short lives. It's inspiring that they were able to find each other and form a loving bond that is evident to anyone who speaks to them. I guess that's not surprising now that we know they are siblings." She paused to smile at them. "I was inclined to grant the permanent custody to Miss Hope Scott even before that information came to light. So congratulations, Levi. Hope Scott is now your official guardian. Good luck to you both."

The gavel sounded and a cheer erupted from behind them.

Hope stood abruptly and pulled Levi into her arms. "We did it, kid. Ready to go home?"

"Home," he echoed with a contented sigh. "You have no idea."

But she did know. She hadn't exactly walked in his shoes when she was his age, but it had been close enough. "Come on." She slipped her arm through his and steered him toward the group of people waiting for them. "That old life, it's gone. It's you and me now. Got it?"

Levi nodded, his hand tightening around hers.

"And me," Chad added, slipping his arm around Hope's shoulders. "And the entire Townsend clan."

Levi laughed as Abby threw her arms around him. "This is your official welcome-to-the-family hug," she said into his ear. "I hope you like having everyone all up in your business, because having five sisters is no joke."

"You can say that again," Yvette added as soon as Abby released him. "Come hang with me, Levi. I'll at least let you disappear into the stacks at my bookstore while making the easiest paycheck around."

"Yeah. Easy right up until half the state descends on the place for one of your over-the-top book signings." Noel rolled her eyes. "I'm sure he'd rather help at the inn during those busy weekends. After this baby is born, I'm definitely going to need another pair of hands around the place. Besides, the tips are phenomenal."

"Or," Abby added. "He can just help me package up my products in my studio and not have to deal with anyone in customer service."

Everyone turned to Faith, waiting to see what kind of job she was going to offer him. She laughed and held up her hands. "I'm not sure we can compete with that." Smiling, she tugged him away from Yvette and said, "How about you just come see me when you're tired of those three taking advantage of your cheap labor. We'll hang by the fire pit, and I'll teach you how to play pool and darts and anything else the cool aunts do."

Levi leaned into her. "I think you're my favorite already." But even as he said the words, his gaze landed on Hope, and the love that shone back at her made her nearly melt right there. Her heart was full as she watched her sisters shuffle Levi out of the courthouse and make plans for a celebration party.

"Looks like you officially have a teenager," Chad said, his hand slipping down to rest on the small of her back.

She glanced up at him, unable to keep from grinning like a fool. "Looks like it." Then her smile faded as she voiced the tiny fear that had been niggling at the back of her mind. "What do you think? Is it too much pressure dating a girl who has a teenager?"

His eyebrows shot up his forehead. "Have you really been worried about that?"

She shrugged. Despite the date they'd made for that Thursday morning last week, they still hadn't found any time to be alone together, and she was starting to wonder if he was going to get frustrated. "My life isn't exactly uncomplicated."

"It's not complicated, Hope. It's full of love and family," he said, guiding her out of the building and over to a corner where they'd have some privacy. "What's not to like about that?"

She pressed a hand to his cheek. "How is it that you're so wonderful? You always know exactly the right thing to say."

"Not always," he said, his face tightening as he glanced down.

She frowned. "Like when?"

He gave her a small smile, vulnerability shining in those

gorgeous blue eyes of his. "Like right now when all I want to do is ask you something, but I'm a thousand percent certain it's too soon."

Hope stopped breathing as she stared up at him. He didn't mean what she thought he meant, did he? Forcing herself to take a breath, she said, "I think you should just ask me."

His blue gaze searched her green one, and whatever he saw there seemed to give him confidence, because an easy smile claimed his lips as he dug something out of his pocket. Holding her left hand in his, he said, "I've been carrying this ring around with me ever since the day we decided to be exclusive."

Hope's gaze locked onto the antique diamond ring he was holding at the tip of her ring finger. Was this really happening? Should she be letting this happen? They had only been dating for a little over a month, but she'd been in love with him for over three years. For her, there was no question what she wanted. All she wanted was Chad.

"I knew for sure it was way too soon to be talking about marriage. It's too soon now by most people's standards. But the thing is, Hope, I've cared about you for a very long time. I've held you in my heart since the last time I saw you in Berkeley, and since the moment I ran into you here in Keating Hollow, my heart has belonged to you. I'm certain that I'm in love with you, and if it's possible, I'm even more certain that I want us to be a family. You, me, and Levi. I don't want to leave your house every night. I want to be there in the morning when you wake up. I want to kiss you whenever I think about it and make love to you deep into the night. But most of all, I just want to live my life by your side, grow old with you, and never, ever be separated again."

Happy, joyful tears streamed down her face. His words, *I want us to be a family*, echoed in her mind over and over again.

Family was the one thing she'd wanted as a kid. And now she had it in spades. But the idea of Chad being a part of that family... it wasn't something she'd really allowed herself to think about yet. But now that he'd put it out there, her mind had latched on and wasn't going to let go. "Yes," she said enthusiastically. "Absolutely yes, I want you, me, and Levi to be a family. The sooner the better."

Relief flooded his blue eyes, and he let out the breath he'd been holding as he slid the ring onto her finger. "Hope Scott, will you marry me?"

"A million times yes, Chad Garber. Yes."

His grin lit up his face as he wrapped his arms around her and spun her around to a chorus of cheers from the Townsends and Levi, who clapped loudly and wolf-whistled when Chad's lips crashed down on hers.

"I guess the secret's already out," he whispered when they broke apart.

"I guess this means you can stay the night tonight," she countered and pulled him back down for another searing kiss.

CHAPTER 31

*S*hannon Ansell fussed with the chocolate display in the far corner of the music shop, trying to ignore the fact that Brian Knox had just walked in. It was the grand opening of Magical Notes, Chad Garber's new store on Main Street, and she'd been asked to cater the desserts. She'd been more than happy to provide chocolate from a Spoonful of Magic... right up until she realized that Brian Knox was slotted as the entertainment.

Why did he have to be there, looking hotter than ever in his low-slung jeans and skin-tight black T-shirt? All she could think about when she looked at him was that disastrous night when she'd agreed to go out with him that had ended up with her in his bed and him scrambling out of it. Her face heated just thinking about it. If it was possible to die of embarrassment, she'd have keeled over already. But no. She was very much alive and so was he. And now she had no choice but to face the music, so to speak. Or maybe she could just slip out the back without anyone noticing.

"Shannon!" Hope Scott called as she made her way to the

back of the store. Her blond hair was piled on the top of her head in a sophisticated bun, and she was wearing a formfitting jumpsuit that showed off all her curves. Ever since the woman had gotten engaged to Chad, she'd just radiated happiness. If Shannon didn't already know the woman deserved every last bit of joy after everything she'd been through, she'd almost hate her for it. Instead, seeing Hope so happy filled Shannon's heart with a lightness that was unfamiliar and welcome at the same time. "These chocolate-covered caramel squares are to die for. Are they a new recipe?"

Shannon smiled at her. "Yep. I made them just for this event. Chad said you were a big fan of unusual flavors, so I went to work and came up with something a little different."

She took another bite. "Ginger and...?"

"Cardamom. It gives it a little something extra, I think," Shannon said.

"Definitely." Hope grabbed a couple more caramels and made her way back over to Chad, who was busy showing a baby grand to one of the seasonal residents of Keating Hollow.

"Hello there, gorgeous," a rich, seductive voice said from behind her.

Shannon froze. Brian. *Dammit.* There was no escaping now. She swallowed her unease and turned around, giving him a smirk. "Brian. Nice of you to finally show your face."

"Was I hiding?" he asked, raising his eyebrows.

"I don't know. Were you? Seems like I haven't seen you around for weeks. My phone didn't ring for that second date you asked for either." The words were out of her mouth before she could stop them. Why had she said that? Hadn't she told herself she was going to pretend nothing had happened? That he hadn't taken her out, given her the best kiss of her life, promised to take her out again the next week, and then rejected her wholesale when she'd all but thrown herself at him two hours later. Her inner voice scoffed at her. There was no "all but" about it. She'd unabashedly thrown herself at him and had walked away with a bruise on her ego so big that she'd decided to swear off men for good.

His mouth worked, but no words came out.

Ha, she thought. The sophisticated man from Los Angeles didn't know how to respond when he was called out on his BS. Well good. She had no time for games anyway. "Never mind." She waved an unconcerned hand. "That's all water under the bridge anyway. It was good to see you again, Brian." She started to walk off but was stopped when he reached out and lightly grabbed her arm.

"Wait just a second," he said, moving in close so that his chest brushed her back. "About that night—"

She jerked away. "There's no need to explain, Brian. I got the message loud and clear. Forget I said anything." She forced a smile and strode into the back room, pretending she needed to restock supplies. Instead, she leaned against the storage shelves and took in a deep breath. Brian Knox was everything she'd ever craved. Tall, dark, and handsome didn't begin to cover it. He was also smart, funny, flirty, and full of confidence. He had it all and he knew it. He was just the type of guy that could curl her toes and make her heart melt, only to walk away three months later when someone sweeter and more innocent walked into his life.

Shannon was the type of girl guys like him wanted to date, not marry. And Shannon was looking for a partner to raise a family. A bed buddy was not on the agenda, despite the fact that her earlier actions had contradicted that fact.

Footsteps sounded on the concrete floor.

Shannon pushed away from the shelves and straightened

her shoulders, an excuse for being in the back room already forming on her tongue. Only it wasn't Chad or Hope or Levi coming to check on her. It was Brian. She bit back a scowl.

"What are you doing back here?" she asked.

"Looking for you." He stepped in front of her, trapping her between his muscular body and the shelves.

She looked up and noted the scar running through one of his eyebrows and almost licked her lips. Dammit. Why did he have to push all of her buttons just by existing? "Well, you found me. What did you want?"

"That second date," he said without hesitation.

"Why?" she said with a sigh, suddenly very tired.

"Why?" he asked with a chuckle. "You're kidding, right?" He let his gaze sweep over her body, lingering on her cleavage and then moving to her legs before finally landing on her lips. "You're the most gorgeous creature in this town. Don't you think I kick myself every time I think about that night? I want another shot with you, Shannon. Let me make it up to you. Let me take you out on Friday night."

She should have been flattered, but she wasn't. Shannon knew she had a body that looked amazing in a cocktail dress. She wasn't blind to the attention she'd received over the years. Her thirty-four double-Ds combined with her hourglass figure had garnered her a lot of advances over the years. Most of them because the men in question only saw her body and nothing else.

Unfortunately, she suspected Brian had fallen under the same spell. He regretted turning her down and hadn't been able to stop thinking about what it might've been like. So here he was to collect. Only her offer had long since expired. "Sorry, Brian. Ask me again when you're interested in more than just my body."

"That's not why I'm asking you out," he said firmly.

She raised one eyebrow. "Really? You just looked at me like you wanted to eat me before staring at my mouth. It sure looks like it from here."

The tips of his ears turned bright pink, and she knew she'd hit the nail on the head. Very gently, she pressed her palm to his chest and pushed him away. He didn't resist, and she slipped away from him, striding toward the door without another word.

"Shannon?" he said.

She paused in the doorway, glancing back at him. "Yes?"

"I'm going to prove you wrong."

She chuckled. "Oh? Wanna bet on it?"

His easy gaze turned determined as he took a few steps toward her. "Name your terms."

Was he for real? She still didn't believe that he was interested in anything more than just a roll in the hay, but she couldn't resist a good bet. So she cocked her head to the side and said, "All right. Six dates in six weeks. You have to plan them all around things that I enjoy. It's your job to figure that out. If any of the dates go sideways, it's over and you have to be my pool boy until the end of October when we get around to winterizing it, and your uniform will consist of a thong."

Brian's eyes gleamed at the suggestion. "A thong is awfully uncomfortable, Shannon. And isn't that a little late to be winterizing a pool around here?"

"The pool has been spelled to withstand the cooler temps. No need to worry about that. Though you might be cold wandering around mostly naked," she said with a snicker. "And I'm aware thongs are uncomfortable. But now I'm wondering when and why you were ever wearing one."

He winked. "I'll tell you when I win the bet. Now, if I win, you have to agree to attend my sister's wedding as my fiancée and give me a two-hour body massage. We'll both be completely naked."

She blinked at him. "You can't be serious. Why would you want me to pretend to be your fiancée?"

"Who said anything about pretending?" he said with a grin. "What do you say?"

Her head screamed at her to say no. This was a crazy bet that was bound to trample her heart one way or another. She'd given up on men like Brian who said things they didn't mean and messed with her head. But she had never been one for going the safe route. And everything inside of her craved Brian Knox. She couldn't say no. Her mouth wouldn't let her. Besides, there was no way he was going to stay interested after six weeks. They never did. Knowing it was a mistake and not caring in the least, she held her hand out and said, "It's a bet."

DEANNA'S BOOK LIST

Pyper Rayne Novels:
Spirits, Stilettos, and a Silver Bustier
Spirits, Rock Stars, and a Midnight Chocolate Bar
Spirits, Beignets, and a Bayou Biker Gang
Spirits, Diamonds, and a Drive-thru Daiquiri Stand
Spirits, Spells, and Wedding Bells

Jade Calhoun Novels:
Haunted on Bourbon Street
Witches of Bourbon Street
Demons of Bourbon Street
Angels of Bourbon Street
Shadows of Bourbon Street
Incubus of Bourbon Street
Bewitched on Bourbon Street
Hexed on Bourbon Street
Dragons of Bourbon Street

Last Witch Standing Novels:

Soulless at Sunset
Bloodlust By Midnight
Bitten At Daybreak

Crescent City Fae Novels:
Influential Magic
Irresistible Magic
Intoxicating Magic

Witches of Keating Hollow Novels:
Soul of the Witch
Heart of the Witch
Spirit of the Witch
Dreams of the Witch
Courage of the Witch
Love of the Witch
Power of the Witch

Witch Island Brides:
The Vampire's Last Dance
The Wolf's New Year Bride
The Warlock's Enchanted Kiss
The Shifter's First Bite

Destiny Novels:
Defining Destiny
Accepting Fate

ABOUT THE AUTHOR

New York Times and USA Today bestselling author, Deanna Chase, is a native Californian, transplanted to the slower paced lifestyle of southeastern Louisiana. When she isn't writing, she is often goofing off with her husband in New Orleans or playing with her two shih tzu dogs. For more information and updates on newest releases visit her website at deannachase.com.

Made in the USA
Middletown, DE
22 October 2023

41256175R00154